LOVING LONDON

ELLIE WADE

OTHER TITLES BY ELLIE WADE

Forever Baby
Fragment
Chasing Memories

THE CHOICES SERIES

A Beautiful Kind of Love
A Forever Kind of Love

THE FLAWED HEART SERIES

Finding London
Keeping London

PLEASE VISIT ELLIE'S AMAZON AUTHOR PAGE FOR MORE
INFORMATION ON HER OTHER BOOKS.

WOULD YOU LIKE TO KNOW WHEN ELLIE HAS
GIVEAWAYS, SALES, OR NEW RELEASES?

SIGN UP FOR HER NEWSLETTER. ♥

Visit my website at www.elliewade.com
Cover Designer: Regina Wamba, Mae-I-Design
Editor and Interior Designer: Jovana Shirley,
Unforeseen Editing, www.unforeseenediting.com

ISBN-13: 978-1539012702

*To all the soldiers who have served in the military
and to the families that love them.*

Thank you.

ONE

Loïc

> *"The utter horror of it all comes back in*
> *agonizing clarity. Cooper's gone."*
> —Loïc Berkeley

Heaviness weighs on me, pressing my lungs flat. I can't breathe. Panic rises within as a war with fear begins.

It's so dark.

Where am I?

It smells but not of earth and sweat. It reeks of chemicals and sanitation—rubbing alcohol maybe.

My chest expands as I pull in air, and it brings torture, a shooting sharp pain to my ribs. I stop inhaling deeply and focus on taking short and shallow breaths.

What's happening to me?

Where am I?

I try to open my eyes, but it becomes way more difficult than it should be. Why won't they open? I mentally instruct my brain to make my eyes open, and I wait.

Open.

Open.

Open.

Nothing happens.

Fuck.

A stabbing agony shoots through my body, starting at my head and spreading downward. The ache in my leg burns so fiercely that I know I'm dying. A pain this great can't be sustained. I scream a hollow, tortured cry, but no sound explodes from me. In fact, I can't hear anything at all.

And the pain...it's just too much.

It's more than I can stand.

I'm dying.

I clench my teeth together and bear down, trying to hold on, to sustain through the anguish.

But I can't.

I'm not strong enough.

I know it's over—life is leaving me—but as darkness pulls me under, I'm grateful for the release.

"Lieutenant Berkeley, can you hear me?" a male voice asks.

It takes me a moment to register the words. I sluggishly open my eyes but force them closed again. The intrusive light hurts.

"Sir?" he questions again.

Breathing deep, I open my eyes again, even more cautiously, allowing them to acclimate to the brightness that surrounds me.

I blink and then blink again.

Scanning the room, I realize I'm in a hospital. *What happened?*

When the man is in my line of vision, I stop my assessment of the room. He looks to be in his forties with kind brown eyes, but if I'm not mistaken, I see pity in them.

Do I? That thought causes bile to rise in my throat. *Why is he looking at me that way?*

Opening my mouth, I try to question him; nothing but a raspy croak comes out.

The man raises a hand. "Your throat's going to be dry. Let me get you some water."

He exits the room, leaving me to myself, as I wade hopelessly through a sea of questions. Closing my eyes, I try to remember what happened. The crazy thing is, I can't remember much of anything. My mind is so clouded, so saturated, with a heavy mud of nothingness.

The man returns, holding a white Styrofoam cup with a straw. He pushes a button on the side of my bed, and the section behind my back starts to slowly move up.

"Is that okay? It doesn't hurt?" he asks.

I shake my head, answering his second question.

He continues moving the back of the bed up until I'm in a seated position. He then holds the cup of water in front of my face, and the bent straw presses against my lips. Opening my lips, I take a sip. The water feels like shards of glass sliding down my throat. I take another sip and then indicate with a nod that I'm finished.

The man places the cup on my side table. "I'm Sergeant Hannigan, your current nurse. Though Private

Taylor will be replacing me"—his eyes dart to the clock on the wall—"in about an hour, and she's much sweeter than I am. Everyone loves her. She's a hell of a lot easier on the eyes, too." He smiles, amused with himself.

"What…" I try to ask.

"Your throat's going to be sore for a bit. Try to keep it hydrated as best as you can. You were intubated for a while. Then, you were in a medically induced coma until the swelling in your brain went down and your major injuries healed some. Do you remember what happened?"

I shake my head.

"Well, you're at Landstuhl Regional Medical Center in Germany," he says.

Immediately, I recognize that as the military hospital where soldiers injured overseas are sent for medical attention.

He continues, "You were in Afghanistan. On a mission to Sarowbi, you were hit by shrapnel caused by a grenade, and the explosion propelled you into a wall, which you hit pretty hard. You were evacuated and flown here. From what I hear, you're lucky to be alive."

"Injuries?" I manage to say.

"You had some head trauma and many lacerations that needed stitches. You took some shrapnel in the side of your abdomen, but luckily, it missed all your major organs."

I catch him swiftly looking down before his gaze returns to mine.

"A large piece of shrapnel struck your left leg, causing a significant amount of damage. The surgeon had to amputate part of your leg, starting right above the knee."

My eyes bulge as I take in his words. *Amputate?*

Warily, I peer down toward the bedding that covers me. Sure enough, the thin white sheet drops down to the mattress where my lower left leg should be.

I lift my arm to move the covers from me but gasp as an acute pain hits, radiating from my rib area. I press my arm below my chest until the ache recedes.

"I'm sorry. I forgot to tell you about your broken ribs. Your body's still pretty bruised up. It will be a while before you're healed."

I nod toward my leg. "Can I see it?" My voice cracks.

"Sure." Sergeant Hannigan pulls back the sheet.

From beneath the hospital gown I'm wearing, my right leg lays in shades of bruises against the mattress. It's like a messed up tie-dye of purples, yellows, and browns with some cuts thrown in the mix for variety. It's almost nauseating in appearance.

Then, I steel the nerve to take in my left leg, and...it's gone.

Just gone.

My gaze returns to the bruised up appendage and then to the spot beside it where its counterpart should be, and nothing is there. Nothing. No matching mangled up leg is protruding from beneath the thin gown.

As I stare at the spot where my leg should be, Sergeant Hannigan pulls up the gown a few inches to reveal the bandaged up stump of my left leg. There's really nothing to see, except a gauzed up nub, the pathetic remnant of a leg.

Letting out a sigh, I lean my head back against the pillow. The sergeant fixes my bedding back around me.

I close my eyes and think about my legs, and the crazy thing is, I can still feel the left one. I can actually feel it. I move my foot around in a circle, taking in the way my ankle cracks with the motion. Yet, when I open my eyes and peer down, there's no left foot to move. I simply stare at the spot where it should be.

"Are you okay, Lieutenant?" Hannigan asks.

"I'm fine," I lie. How can I be okay? I'm banged up as hell, in a hospital in Germany, without a fucking leg. No, I'm not fine.

"I know this is a lot to take in. We have doctors you can talk to. It helps."

"No, I'm okay, really." I turn my head to the side and notice the window for the first time. Unfortunately, my view is of brown bricks, more than likely the exterior from another part of the hospital.

"All right, well, I'm going to finish up your chart. Private Taylor will be here soon, and she'll order some soft foods for you, so your body can get used to eating solids again. Nothing says dinner like Jell-O, right?" Hannigan's question is rhetorical, so I ignore it. "The doctor will be here sometime within the next hour to go over everything with you as well. I paged him when you started to wake up. Can I get you anything before I go?"

"No," I answer quietly.

"Okay, if you need anything, just press this call light right here." He shows me the red button on the railing. "I just pushed some pain meds through your IV right before you woke up, but if the pain becomes too much, we can give you some more."

"Oh, Sergeant Hannigan?" I say before he leaves.

He turns to look at me. "Yeah?"

"How long have I been here?"

"About two weeks."

"How long do you think I'll stay here?" I ask.

"You can talk to the doctor when he gets in, but I'm guessing you'll be here for another two weeks before you're well enough to fly to Walter Reed, the big military hospital in Washington DC. There, you'll probably have intense PT for about a month before they clear you to go home and get the rest of your treatment at the nearest VA hospital to you. So, that will put you home sometime in May. Things can vary, of course, but given an injury like yours, that's my guess," he says cheerfully.

"Thanks." I nod.

He smiles warmly and exits the room.

Feeling tired, I close my eyes. I can figure this all out later—reconstruct the pieces of my life, regain my memories, discover how to do all the things I love with one leg. Right now though, I just need to sleep.

Whether from the pain meds or the sheer exhaustion of my battered body, sleep takes me almost instantly. I'm on the precipice of blissful deep slumber—in that moment right before the entire world fades away but where I'm still subconsciously aware of where my physical body lies—when it happens.

I see *him*.

I watch in a panic as he jumps, throwing his body over the grenade.

I try to stop him, but I can't. I can't reach him in time.

I stare in horror as his body explodes. Pieces of his body hit me as they fly through the air, and I scream out in pain—an unrelenting, intense agony so deep that it burns clear through to my soul.

The utter horror of it all comes back in agonizing clarity.

Cooper's gone.

He's gone.

I bolt up in bed, immune to the screeching protests of my body, and I yell, a wild cry from the worst pain I've ever known.

I can't stop screaming. The heartache is killing me. It's so tangible that it manifests as physical pain, ripping through me, breaking my mind, body, and soul into thousands of empty pieces.

I vaguely register the presence of others. Somewhere in the distance, I hear my name being called, but I can't get back there.

I'm drowning in a sea of suffering. Visions of Cooper's tattered body hit me with the force of massive rocks, carved out from a mountain of torment. I can feel the weight of it crushing me to the ground. The earth beneath me shakes with anger. It's taking me with it. I'm going to be buried alive in my own misery, and I deserve it.

It shouldn't have been him.

Not him.

Never him.

Suddenly, the yelling stops, and I'm enveloped in blackness. My mind is foggy, and I can't focus on the images of Cooper. I'm losing him.

I can't...

I've already...

Lost.

Him.

TWO

Loïc

"I realize that I'm barely more than a pile of wasted matter as it is, but I exist. At least that's something."
—Loïc Berkeley

I've been living in déjà vu hell for the past week.

I wake. I remember Cooper. I freak out. I'm drugged. I sleep.

And repeat.

In the few lucid moments before said freak-outs occur, I remember everything. All my memories, for good or bad, have returned.

The shitty thing is, most of my memories fucking suck. I've had a miserable life. I lose everything that I love. Everything. A constant nightmare reel is playing in my mind—to torment me, I suppose. I've been lying in this bed, unable to escape, and forced to relive all my horrific experiences…over and over and over again.

Fleeting visions of London try to break through all the ugly, but I don't let her. In fact, thinking about her just pisses me off because I know I can never have her. I will lose her, just like everyone else. I'm not going to wait around for that torturous experience to happen. It all ends now.

I was wrong to let Cooper in. I should have known.

But I won't take London down with me.

It's been three weeks since I've been in contact with London. Who knows? She might have already moved on. It's for the best if she has.

Another week has passed. Seven days. One hundred sixty-eight hours. Ten thousand eighty minutes. Each moment passes by like a gray fog, enveloping me in its nothingness.

And that's what I feel—absolutely nothing. I'm a hollow waste of space.

I no longer jolt awake from my nightmares to find myself screaming in agony until a nurse rushes in with sedatives to calm my cries. Then again, I've been finding it difficult to experience any feelings at all. The medical staff has thrown around terms like *depression and post-traumatic stress disorder*, or PTSD. I've been taking more pills daily than is probably healthy, but I can't find it in me to care about that either.

The truth of it is, I've lost all my desire—to live, to feel, to love, to care. It's just gone. Whether from a high dose of medications or as a result of my circumstances and mental state, I don't know, and it doesn't matter anyway. I don't want to feel, care, or love. *Why would I?* It causes nothing but heartbreak. I've had enough hurt for multiple lifetimes.

I realize that I'm barely more than a pile of wasted matter as it is, but I exist. At least that's something.

I couldn't physically sustain any more. I'd crumble. Another blow that causes me emotional pain would end me. It'd be over. I know it. I've lost all my fight. Simply existing is enough of a struggle. It's all I can manage.

Blinking, I escape from my thoughts and focus again on what the doctor sitting beside my bed is saying. All right, so I don't focus on her *words* per se. I watch as her lips move, noticing the wrinkles beside her mouth shift and bend with each word. She must be at least fifty, maybe even sixty. Her face wears the wrinkles of life well. They're not deep and weathered, like someone who's suffered. They're fine and delicate, like someone who's lived and aged gracefully. I would bet that she's had a good life. Her eyes are dark brown, and they shine with happiness. They remind me of another's eyes, of a beautiful girl I used to love, but I push that thought down deep, where I won't have to confront it.

What's her name again?

Dr. W-something. Maybe Wayne? Washington? White?

I can't remember even though she's come to see me every day for the past week. My gaze drops to the badge she wears. Squinting, I read, *Dr. Olivia Warner.*

That's it.

Dr. Warner has been more than patient with me. Frankly, I'm not sure why she keeps coming. It has to be clear that I'm not really listening to her. I barely speak in our sessions. I don't want to participate in this psychoanalytical shit that she's attempting. I have no desire to break down my walls, face my fears, or anything

11

of the sort. I certainly don't want to talk about any of it. I'm content to remain in my state of empty existence.

"Loïc?" Her voice is louder than normal with a persistent tone.

It startles me enough to break my stare that was analyzing her pink silk blouse. I snap my eyes up to meet her expectant gaze.

"I said, have you contacted any of your loved ones, like we spoke about?"

I simply gape at her.

"Loïc, it's important for your recovery. You need to feel that connection with people who care about you. There's a life waiting for you back home. It's crucial that you remind yourself of that. Can you please try to contact someone from home? A call would be best, but you can start with an email if that makes you more comfortable. Would you like me to help you?"

I shake my head. "I can do it."

Dr. Warner lets out a breath of relief. It isn't often that I respond to one of her questions. I suppose it's only fair that I give her this small victory.

"That's great, Loïc. I promise you, it will help you heal. It's so important for you to realize that you have so much to live for." She smiles, and a warm kindness exudes from her. I know she means well. "As you know, this is our last session. My colleague, Dr. Benjamin, will be continuing your therapy while you're at Walter Reed. He's a wonderful man."

I nod even though I couldn't care less who'll be taking her place.

Dr. Warner talks for a while longer, little of which I actually hear, before she smiles at me one last time and exits my room.

Tomorrow, I will be flying back to the States. I'll be getting a prosthetic leg, several new doctors, and a new regimen of therapies, both physical and psychological. I don't know how to feel about it all, so I suppose I'll continue feeling nothing.

THREE

Loïc

"I feel nothing."
—*Loïc Berkeley*

"There you go, Berk! You're kicking ass today," Lieutenant Dixon, my physical therapist, cheers.

"I'm kicking a ball, Dick, not fighting in an MMA competition," I say in a grumpy tone with an immature roll of my eyes.

Truth is, Dixon—whom I've called Dick for the past month—is my favorite person here. I've been an asshole to him from day one, and he's been nothing but supportive. He held a one-sided conversation with me for the first week of physical therapy until I finally started to respond. He's upbeat, crude, and funny, and damn it if he doesn't remind me so much of Cooper. I hate that as much as I love that about him. Regardless, I can't help but like him.

"And you're kicking the shit out of that ball. If it weren't for the obvious metal appendage, I might mistake you for David Beckham."

"You're an ass." I manage a small grin as I kick the large ball with a force equivalent to a five-year-old and certainly not a world-class soccer player.

Dixon says that I'm physically bouncing back quicker than most soldiers do. I spend the majority of my time working out, completing the regimen that Dixon has prescribed me. I always do at least double the repetitions or twice the amount of time he suggests. If he wants me to do ten lunges, I do twenty, minimum. If he tells me to walk for thirty minutes, I walk for an hour.

My body hurts all the time, but I welcome the pain. It takes my mind off the other hurt, which is much more difficult to bear. I don't have control over a lot anymore. Mentally, I'm weak. My nightmares are debilitating, and my broken heart refuses to heal. But for the most part, I can manage my body. I can strengthen my muscles and improve my coordination. It helps me when I see positive changes in my physical abilities, as it's the only aspect of my life that I seem to have any real control over.

After an hour, I'm drenched in sweat, my muscles are quivering in agony, and I feel better than I have in a long time. I wouldn't say that I'm happy, but I feel a sliver of accomplishment, and that's something to hold on to.

"I have a little over an hour before my next session. You want to meet me in the cafeteria for lunch?" Dixon asks.

I fight my urge to say no. "Yeah. Let me go take a quick shower, and I'll meet you down there."

Dixon nods nonchalantly in approval, but I know he's happy that I accepted. Everyone here is always trying to get me to open up, but I'm a master at keeping people out. I've had a lifetime of practice.

Twenty minutes later, I enter the cafeteria and spot Dixon sitting at a table in the corner of the room. I walk through the food line and grab a large Italian sub, an apple, and a bottle of water. As I walk toward Dixon, carrying my tray of food, I can't help but take note of how far I've come. Two weeks ago, I didn't have the balance to complete a task as simple as walking while holding a tray. I can walk without a cane now, and yes, while it's more of a hobble than a smooth gait, it's impressive because I know how much work it took me to get here.

Placing my tray down, I take a seat across from Dixon as he shovels a forkful of food into his mouth.

"Dude, this meatloaf is on point," Dixon utters through a mouthful of food.

"Yeah, you seem to be thoroughly enjoying it," I state as I lower my gaze to my sub.

"So, how's life, my man? Any news to report?" Dixon asks happily.

"You know I don't have a life."

"Have you spoken with anyone from home?" he inquires casually.

"Come on, Dick. Is lunch going to be a therapy session? Because, if it is, I think I'll pass."

Dixon shrugs his shoulder. "I'm just making small talk."

"*Riiight*," I say sarcastically, drawing out the word.

"You're heading home in a couple of weeks. I was just wondering if you'd had a chance to let anyone back home know."

"You haven't talked to Benjamin by any chance, have you?" I accuse.

My therapist, Dr. Benjamin, has been trying to get me to call home for a month now but to no avail. I know I should. I realize that I have to face that part of my life. But I just feel so mentally and physically broken and hopeless. I haven't been able to find the courage to make a call, let alone check my email.

"Why would you say that?" Dixon asks innocently.

I exhale. "Don't fuck with me, Dick."

Dixon holds up his hands in surrender. "Okay, okay. I might have spoken with Benjamin. He's worried about you, Berk. Frankly, I am, too. If you think you're in a dark place here, wait till you get home. It's worse. The mental shit that comes with PTSD is no joke. That shit can drag you down. Do you know how many brothers' funerals I've attended because they couldn't take it in the real world?"

Dixon's eyes widen with a sadness that pounds me in the gut, almost knocking the wind out of me. He's never been this serious with me, and I'd be lying if I said it wasn't a bit of a reality check.

"I get that you don't like to let people in. You'd prefer to handle everything on your own. But, Berk, man…you need someone, even just one person. I'm telling you, there might be a time when the darkness is too great. It will try to suck you down, to annihilate you. It's crucial that you have someone to help you up when you're too weak to care. I've seen it. This beast has beaten even the strongest of men. You are not immune. And…fuck it. I refuse to attend your funeral, Berkeley. Do you hear me?"

Dixon's words steal my breath, like a bucket of ice water being dumped over my bare skin. His speech, in the corner of this hospital cafeteria, falls somewhere between a scolding and a plea, and it's completely sobering.

"All right, I got it."

18

"Do you?" he questions with an accusing stare.

I nod. "I do. I'll figure it out, okay?"

"Okay." He seems relieved. "Also, when you're home, you'll need to keep up with your doctor appointments, PT, therapy, and your medications. Don't let anything falter because, sometimes, it's impossible to get back."

"I. Got. It." I pin him with a warning stare.

"You'd better," he scoffs. "I'm not going to be there to coax you through your exercises."

I know this is his way of lightening the mood because, if anything, he's had to urge me to hold back during physical therapy.

"I know. How will I ever kick a ball without you?"

"Exactly my point," he huffs out.

"It will be rough, but I'll find a way," I kid with an exaggerated sigh.

He grins. "I know you will. You're a fighter, man."

Two hours later, I find myself sitting in the cramped computer lab. My hand physically shakes as I type in my Gmail username and password. My heart is thrumming wildly in my chest, and I'm terrified to open my email. Ignoring my life back home has been a coward move, I admit. But the past two months since that grenade took my best friend have been a sort of hell. The first month, I had to fight to hold on to my sanity. The past thirty days, I've immersed myself into healing my physical form so that I wouldn't have to confront the rest.

Honestly, it's much easier to learn to walk with a metal leg than it is to face internal demons. In a battle of strength, a weak mind loses every time. I don't need Dr. Benjamin or anyone else pyschoanalyzing me. I know, inside—where it matters the most—I'm broken.

Closing my eyes, I pull air into my lungs. Releasing the air in a controlled breath, I open my eyes to confront my inbox.

And there they are...

Message after message.

Most are from London. Some are from Maggie. Others are from Sarah. As I scroll down the screen, there's a random email here or there from a brother in my unit. I'm sure, they're checking in on me.

But...the majority is from London.

I start at the bottom, opening the oldest message, which happens to be from London.

To: Loïc Berkeley

From: London Wright

Subject: I'm so sorry.

Loïc,

I just heard about Cooper. I don't know what else to say besides I'm so, so very sorry. I wish I had something to say to make this better, but I know nothing will. I wish more than anything that it hadn't happened. I wish that you didn't have to go through the pain that I know you are feeling. I wish you were here right now, so I could hold you.

I love you, Loïc. We are going to get through this. You are going to get through this.

Please write when you can. I hate that I can't be with you right now.

Are they going to let you come home for the funeral?

I'm sorry. I wish I had something better to say that would help you, but I'm at a loss. All I know is that, as horrible as this is...we will get through it, Loïc. It won't always hurt this much.

I love you.

I'm sorry.

I'm so very sorry.

Love,

London

And I open another.

To: Loïc Berkeley

From: London Wright

Subject: Please call me.

Loïc,

I'm so sorry about Cooper, and I'm so worried about you. Please call me. We can get through this. You can get through this. Talk to me.

I love you.

Love,

London

And another.

To: Loïc Berkeley

From: London Wright

Subject: I love you.

Loïc,

I love you. I love you. I love you.

I can't wait to hold you.

It won't always hurt this much, I promise.

Please call me anytime, day or night. I don't care when. I can't imagine what you're going through, and I just need to talk to you.

Please call me.

I love you so very much.

Love,

London

And another.

To: Loïc Berkeley

From: London Wright

Subject: I'm sorry.

Loïc,

I don't know what you're going through. But I know how much I'm hurting, and I can only imagine that you're hurting more. I wish I could take away your pain. I wish I could change things. But I can't.

I can be here for you and love you. I can promise you that we can get through this.

Please call me. I'm so worried about you.

I love you so much.

Love,

London

I read each email with detached disinterest. I know the words are meant to comfort me. I realize that they should be eliciting some emotion from me. But I feel nothing.

> To: Loïc Berkeley
>
> From: London Wright
>
> Subject: Love
>
> Loïc,
>
> I know I'm probably not saying the right words. I admit that I don't know what to say to ease some of your pain, if that is even possible. But I do know that I love you. While I might not do or say the correct things, I can love you with everything I am.
>
> Love has the power to heal. I know it does.
>
> I know it won't be tomorrow, next month, or maybe not even next year, but I will love you through all the pain until you're able to feel okay. I understand that you will always mourn Cooper, but someday, you'll be able to look back at the good times that you shared. Maybe, someday, every memory you have of him won't be tainted with sadness. Just maybe?
>
> Please call me.

I love you so much.

Love,

London

It's as if the emails are meant for someone else. I feel no attachment to them or to London. My reaction is not normal; I realize this. But what can I do about that?

To: Loïc Berkeley

From: London Wright

Subject: Are you okay?

Loïc,

Are you okay? I mean, I know you're not okay, but you know what I mean.

Where are you? What's going through your mind? Please share your thoughts with me...whatever they are.

I'm sorry if I'm being selfish, but I need to hear from you. Anything. I'm going crazy, not knowing how you are. I'm terrified of you mourning the loss of Cooper over there by yourself.

Why aren't they sending you home? You can't possibly think clearly on missions with everything that's happened. Don't they understand that?

I get that what you're going through is way worse than what I am feeling. But I love you, and I'm worried sick about you. Maggie hasn't heard from you, and I don't know who else to check with.

Please don't shut me out. Please let me help you.

Please. Please. Please. Please. Please.

I love you, Loïc Berkeley, and nothing will ever change that.

Love,

London

I *want* to cry, to scream even. I want to curse God and everyone else who has ever wronged me. Even though I *want* to want that, I don't. I don't care.

To: Loïc Berkeley

From: London Wright

Subject: Funeral

Loïc,

The funeral's tomorrow. Are they going to let you come home for it?

Hopefully, you are already on your way. God, I hope so.

I need to see you. I don't know what else to say besides I love you.

I. Love. You.

Always. Always. Always.

Love,

London

I've read enough. I don't bother to open the rest.

Reading London's emails, I feel like I'm standing outside a window, looking into a life that isn't mine. A faint familiarity is there, a hint of a lost love. But nothing else. Even when she writes of Cooper's funeral, I can't force myself to feel as deeply as I know I should. It's wrong—all of it. I don't want to hurt, but I should be able to feel something. Some connection.

Perhaps the high doses of medications that I'm on have made me numb. It can't be healthy, but the alternative doesn't feel right either. The screaming, crying, and heart-wrenching night terrors that I experienced in Germany almost did me in. I'm grateful to be on medications that stop those agonizing emotions from breaking through.

I think back to what Dixon said about the darkness being too much for some men to withstand.

Will that be me? It definitely could be. What then?

No, maybe my reaction to these emails isn't *normal*, but I'll take it. I'm not physically or mentally ready to be in a relationship—certainly not now and possibly never again.

A part deep within me resonates with some guilt for what I find myself typing out, but it's so small that it's lost before I'm able to truly grasp it.

To: London Wright

From: Loïc Berkeley

Subject: Enough

It's over.

I send the email without thinking twice. London deserves more, but those two words are all I have to give.

I'm surprised she's still waiting. I had expected a Dear John letter, accompanied by, *I'm so sorry. It's me, not you.* Yet what I found was the opposite.

It doesn't matter though. It doesn't take a rocket scientist to realize that London would take one look at my beaten and battered body and walk the other way. She deserves so much more than I could possibly give her.

I quickly read through the rest of the emails, scanning most of them to catch the important details. Maggie says that she's moved out of our house, paid it off, and left it in my name. I suppose it's good that I'll still have somewhere to live when I get back to Michigan.

Sarah's emails babble on about one guy after another, concern for me, condolences about Cooper, and other random crap.

"One person."

That's what Dixon said. I need to find one person.

London's out, for obvious reasons. Maggie's out because she has her own grief to deal with. She doesn't need me piling my shit on her.

So, that leaves Sarah. Sarah will have to be my one person. I don't have many options at this point. I won't mention to Dixon that my person lives about a nineteen-hour car ride away.

I write down Sarah's phone number, which she left in one of her emails. I'm about to sign out when another email comes through.

> **To: Loïc Berkeley**
>
> **From: London Wright**
>
> **Subject: I love you.**
>
> Loïc,
>
> I don't understand what your email means.
>
> We need to talk. I can't imagine what you're going through, but I want to help.
>
> I know that we can get through anything—even this, as long as we're together.
>
> I will never give up on you or us. Please, talk to me. Call me, anytime.
>
> I love you so very much.

Love,

London

"I'm sorry," I whisper before I shut down the computer.

FOUR

Loïc

"The thought of being responsible for another life
sends a wave of panic through me so fierce
that I can barely breathe."
—Loïc Berkeley

I drop my duffel onto the floor with a thud. *Home.* I look around the living room where I shared so many laughs with Cooper and Maggie. I swallow hard at the memories. It's all the same yet so vastly different.

Maggie left all the furniture and knickknacks. To most people's eyes, this space would look like a normal home.

But I see all that's missing, the little personal details.

The socks that were always on the floor at the base of the couch where Cooper had taken them off after a long day at base—he hated the feeling of socks and had an issue with actually putting them in the laundry room—are gone. Maggie's colorful water bottles that used to grace every flat surface of our house—she apparently wanted to make sure she was never more than an arm's reach away from a drink—are missing. The framed pictures of the three of us and those of Maggie and Cooper have all been taken down.

Yeah, this is a house, but it's not my home.

I don't even know what to do with myself. I no longer have a job. I was medically and honorably discharged—aka fired. Apparently, one needs both legs to be able to serve in the military. The closest person that I had to family died. I have no girlfriend and few friends. I'm alone in this space that's haunted with painful memories.

Sighing, I plop down on the couch and grab the remote. I'm pleased when the TV comes on, and I make a mental note to thank Maggie later for keeping the cable hooked up. I sit in front of the television for what must be a few hours. I'm mindlessly flipping channels when there's a knock at the front door.

What the hell?

I stare toward the door, almost convinced that I'm hearing things, when the knock comes again. I get to my feet and steady myself before making my way toward the door. It takes me longer than usual with my prosthetic. Although I've made huge gains since I first attached the light metal piece to my leg, I have a ways to go before I'll be walking at the pace I used to. The pounding gets louder as I amble my way over and turn the lock. I hesitantly open the door and am greeted by Sarah's shining face.

"Loïc!" she shrieks before forcefully throwing her arms around me and pulling me into a tight hug.

"Sarah?" I say as a question as I hug her back. I have to admit, it's good to see a familiar face.

"What are you doing here?" I ask, pulling away from our embrace. That's when I notice her round belly. "Whoa! Are you pregnant?"

"I'm here because you need me. And, yes," she says in response as she comes inside and closes the door behind herself. "I'm starving," she adds.

I follow her as she makes her way to the kitchen and starts opening the cupboards and the refrigerator. "Loïc, you literally have nothing to eat or drink in this entire kitchen."

"There's water." I nod toward the tap.

"Oh my God, I got here just in time." She sighs with a shake of her head.

"I just got back three hours ago," I say in my defense.

"Well, come on. We have tons to talk about, but I can't even think about any of that until I get some food in this belly."

"I'm not going anywhere." I shake my head.

"Come on. It will be fun. What do you think? That Italian place?"

"Sarah, I'm not leaving this house," I say more forcefully. The thought of going out and participating in normal life around strangers makes me anxious. I'm just not ready.

"All right, grumpy pants. I'll order a pizza, salad, and some pop for delivery. Then, I'll go grocery shopping later. Okay?"

I nod in agreement. Now that she mentions it, I am pretty hungry.

Sarah calls the pizza place and places our order. Then, she heads back outside with a, "I'll be right back."

A minute later, she's dragging two large suitcases through the front door. I stare at the huge bags as she says, "I'll get the rest later. What I really need is to take a shower and brush my teeth. I've been driving for the past nineteen hours. I'm severely gross at the moment. So, I'm assuming I'll be taking Cooper and Maggie's old room?"

My gaze jumps from her bags to her face. "Sarah, what are you doing?"

"Um, unloading my car." She looks at me with a squint. "What do you think I'm doing?"

I run my fingers through my longer than normal hair. "I'm honestly not sure," I respond with a scoff. "Can we sit and talk for a minute?"

She releases the hold on her suitcases and brings a hand up to my shoulder. As she rubs gently, she says, "Of course."

We take a seat on the couch.

"Seriously, I feel like I'm not understanding something. I'm happy to see you, of course. But why are you here?" I ask.

Sarah leans back a fraction, looking shocked. "Because you are," she states simply.

I let out a sigh. "You've got to give me something. I feel like you're talking in code. Why are you here? How long are you staying? Spill the details, please, without making me pry them out of you," I say, attempting not to sound completely annoyed. "And, holy hell, the baby?" I motion toward her round belly. "What is going on?"

"I always said that, when you got back from Afghanistan, I was going to move up to Michigan to live close to you. When you called a couple of weeks ago, you told me that you were getting back today. I just assumed that, since you now live here alone, I would just stay here with you for the time being. I mean, I can find a place of my own after I get a job, if you want. But I really think it's best that I live here with you. I can help you."

I stop her. "I don't need your help, Sarah."

"Just…" She holds up a hand to stop me. "You do need me. You need someone, Loïc. Please don't push me away because you're too stubborn for your own good. You might think you don't need anyone, but you do. Everyone needs someone." Her blue eyes scan my body, and her stare falls on my metal leg that's visible beneath my shorts.

I explained everything to her when I called her from Walter Reed, including the injury to my leg. Yet I'm sure that seeing it and hearing about it are two different things.

"I'm not in a good place right now. I'm no fun to be around. I'm simply…" I let out a pained breath. There's so much I want to say, but I can't find the words for any of it.

"I don't care. I will be here for you. I love you, Loïc. You've always been there for me, even when I was at my worst. *Especially* when I was at my worst." She shakes her head, as if to ward off horrible memories from the past. "You saved me over and over again. I wouldn't be here without you." Her voice falters as her eyes shine with unshed tears.

"But—" I start to say.

She cuts in before I can finish my thought, "I can't imagine what you've been through in the past six months. I've read up a little on PTSD. I Googled news articles about other soldiers who went through similar experiences as you." Her eyes drop again to my leg before she darts them back up to my face. "I know I won't be perfect. I'll make mistakes, probably most of the time, but I'm going to try my hardest to be the person you need."

"I'm not in a good place, Sarah," I state again, putting emphasis on each word.

She places her hand on my good knee. "And that's why you need me. Listen, you loved me and took care of me. It's my turn to take care of you. Do you understand? Let me love you, Loïc. Please let me stay," she pleads.

"Of course you can stay. That's not the issue. I just don't want you to feel obligated to take care of me. I'm fine on my own."

"I know you are." She smiles. "You're the strongest person I know. I want to be here for you. I need to help you. Think of it like you're doing me a favor." She winks, and it brings a small smile to my face.

I nod my head. "Okay, fine. On one condition."

"What's that?" she asks eagerly.

"Tell me what the hell is up with your round belly."

"Oh, right." She giggles. "Well, I'm pregnant."

"We covered that."

She bites her lip before saying, "I'm not completely sure who the father is although I'm pretty confident it's a one-night stand I had."

"Does he know?"

She shakes her head. "No. I don't even know his last name or where he's from. I seriously know zero about the dude. I was quite tipsy when we hooked up. I don't remember much of it."

"Do you think he lives in Orlando?"

She shrugs. "Maybe, but Orlando's a pretty big place. Plus, it gets tons of tourists every day, so he could be from anywhere really. What am I going to do? Put out an ad that states, *Wanted: A man who banged a blonde chick that he met at a bar in Orlando in November*?"

"So, he never told you his name?"

"I'm sure he did. I just don't remember. I didn't think twice about him until I found out I was pregnant and did the math. But, by that time, I couldn't recall any of the details."

"Huh," I say for lack of anything better.

"Yeah." Sarah chuckles. "It's fine. So, anyway, it's a boy, and he's due in August. I'm a little over six months along now."

"Wow, you're going to be a mom." Though I've been in the presence of her belly for a few minutes now, it's still surreal to think about.

"I know. It's insane. I still can't believe it. It's like I won't truly be able to grasp it until I'm holding him in my arms. I'm hoping that I can stay once the baby's born?"

"Of course. You know you're always welcome here. I was just a little shocked to see you earlier, is all."

"Great!" She claps her hands together. "I think it's going to be wonderful with the three of us living here. We'll be like a family."

"Yeah." I nod. A mere ten minutes ago, I was living alone, and now, I've got a family. I'm not sure how to feel about it all just yet, but it doesn't matter anyway. I would never turn Sarah away. "I suppose it'll be cool, being Uncle Loïc." Yet, even as I say it, the thought of being responsible for another life sends a wave of panic through me so fierce that I can barely breathe.

There's a knock at the door, and Sarah jumps up to go get the pizza.

"It's going to be awesome!" she calls back over her shoulder.

Closing my eyes, I focus on my breathing and try to calm my anxiety, so I won't go into a full-blown panic attack. When Sarah returns with the food, I manage to smile at her through the ache in my chest.

"So, I was thinking that I'd take Maggie and Cooper's room, and the baby can have the spare room since it's the smallest. Is that okay?" she asks as she dishes up our plates.

"It's fine."

Truthfully, I don't like the idea of Sarah staying in Cooper's old room, but it's not like I'm going to go in there. It doesn't make sense to leave it empty when there's a need for it. Yet it just hurts to think about.

"This is so great, Loïc. Everything's going to be wonderful. It's like we were always meant to be a family, you know?"

No, I don't know. But I don't know much of anything right now.

FIVE

Loïc

*"London's gone. That thought is as equally
depressing as it is satisfying, but truthfully,
all I can feel is relief."*
—Loïc Berkeley

Look at me. I've been lying on this couch for five, maybe six hours. Is this what my life has come to? *Jeopardy!* plays on the TV before me, but I haven't listened to a word of it. *I'll take Life of a Disabled Veteran for $300, Alex.*

Not even the sight of Alex Trebek, who will always remind me of sweet Mrs. Peters, brings a sliver of joy to my current situation. Mrs. Peters was a kind old lady who made the best cookies. I stayed with her for a brief time when I was a teen. She was the best placement I had growing up, and what I remember most about her— besides her cookies—was her love for Alex Trebek.

Yet the warm nostalgic feelings toward Mrs. Peters aren't returning.

I've been back a week, and my life has been nothing but a black hole of emptiness, even with Sarah frolicking around in a constant state of happiness.

Sarah has been gone for the afternoon, looking for jobs. It's nice to have the place to myself for a while. I love Sarah, I do, but having her here is exhausting. She constantly wants to talk, and if I don't respond with something, she starts getting worried and suggests we go see my doctor at the VA hospital.

No, thank you.

I had two months of therapy, and it was sufficient to last a lifetime. I'm just in a funk. It will pass. Of course I'm going to have an adjustment period as I transition to my new normal. I'll be fine.

There's a knock on the front door. I ignore it. Sarah has a key, so I know it's not her, and I don't want to talk to anyone else. Another knock sounds, followed by the sound of a key turning in the lock.

"Loïc?" Maggie's timid voice resonates from the foyer.

It brings a deep ache to my chest. I will never be able to see or hear Maggie without thinking of Cooper.

I draw in a deep breath, attempting to steady my voice. "In here."

Maggie walks into the living room. The second she sees me, tears begin to fall from her face, and she runs over to me. I sit up just as she wraps me in a hug. Holding me tight, she cries into my shoulder.

I hug her, rubbing her back, as she continues to sob.

"It's okay," I say even though I'm not exactly sure what that means. It sounds like the right thing to say to someone who's grieving. Yet I know that what Maggie's feeling is so much more than grief. And the fact is, I'm not sure anything is okay. Life is kind of messed up right now.

"I didn't know you were back. How long have you been here?" she chokes out as she pulls away from our embrace.

"Almost a week," I answer guiltily, knowing I should have called her. I was a coward.

"I had no idea. I stop by every once in a while to check on the house and get any random mail. I can't believe you're here." She pulls her hands across her face, wiping the tears.

"I'm sorry. I should have called you. I've been having a difficult time with adjusting, I guess."

"Are you okay?" Maggie asks, concerned, as she begins to scan my body. "Oh my gosh." Her voice is high-pitched as the palm of her hand runs over the scars on my arms. She gently grasps the metal hinge that is now my new knee as her chest heaves with fresh tears.

"I'm fine, Mags. I promise." I put my hand atop hers. "I'm okay. Please don't cry for me."

She lifts her woeful gaze up to mine. "I'm so sorry, Loïc. I'm sorry you got hurt. I'm sorry you lost David." Her voice breaks as she says Cooper's first name.

"I know. Me, too. I'm so sorry you lost him, Maggie. I would do anything to change it if I could."

Maggie sits up next to me on the couch. I wrap my arm around her, and she leans her face against my chest. I hold her as she cries, and we mourn him together.

"Were you there when it happened? Is that how you got hurt?"

"Yeah." I nod, trying to block out the visions of Cooper's last few seconds on earth. "I was there."

"I know you're probably not ready to talk about it, and honestly, I don't think I'm ready to hear it. But, someday, will you tell me about his time over there—his last day, his last moments?"

"Someday..." My voice trails off. "Just know that he died a hero, Maggie, and that he loved you. He loved you more than anything."

"I know he did," she says sadly. "It's so unfair, you know?"

"It is," I agree. "It is."

The two of us hold each other within this space that contains years of memories, countless ghosts of Cooper's past, of our past. It's sobering. We're two completely shattered people, Maggie and me. My chest aches for her grief as much as it does for my own, more so honestly. She deserves better than this. So did Cooper.

Maggie and I continue to sit in our embrace. Many minutes pass. The only sounds that echo through the room are Maggie's tears and our collective breaths of sorrow.

Maggie's the first to speak again, "Have you seen London?"

"No," I answer simply.

She sits up to face me. "Why not?"

Closing my eyes, I shake my head. When I open my eyes to find Maggie's stare, I hope she can see the reasons in my gaze because I don't have the words to explain them.

"I just can't."

"She loves you, Loïc."

"I know, but I just can't right now." I let out a sigh.

"You can't shut out the people who love you, Loïc. She can help you through this transition. She's going crazy, not knowing if you're okay. You owe her some sort of explanation."

"I know," I say softly. I know it's true, but I'm not strong enough to confront London right now.

"If you talk with her, maybe see her, you'll see. All the feelings and reasons you two were together will come back. I know it's hard, adjusting back into civilian life, but I don't think it's going to be as difficult as you think. Sometimes, we psych ourselves up for something that we fear, but when we face it, we realize that the reality isn't as hard as we thought it would be. You know?" she asks hopefully.

"Okay." I nod because I don't want to upset Maggie.

"Oh, gosh, I have to go," Maggie says suddenly as she looks down at her watch. "I'm working tonight. I've been picking up a lot of overtime lately. Gives me something to keep my mind busy." She shrugs. "I love you, and I will call you soon. You let me know if you need anything. Call me day or night. Promise?"

"I promise. I love you, too."

She stands from the couch and then turns around to face me. Bending, she plants a soft kiss on my cheek. "I'm so glad you made it home, Loïc. You're going to be okay."

She smiles weakly and then leaves.

I admit that I was dreading seeing Maggie—not because I don't love her, but because I've felt so guilty that I came home instead of Cooper. For some reason, I thought she would resent me for it. Who knows? Maybe she does. She'd never tell me if she did.

I realize that *Jeopardy!* has long been over, not that I was really watching it anyway. I turn the TV off and opt to stare at the blank screen instead. Too many thoughts are running through my brain for me to be able to concentrate on television anyway.

Minutes later, Sarah gets back, carrying loads of grocery bags.

"I'm back, and I got lots of groceries. We have several options for dinner," she says excitedly. "How was your day?"

"Fine. Yours?"

"Oh, it was great! I applied to several restaurants and bars. I'm sure I'll get a job at one of them."

"Good."

Sarah calls from the kitchen, "So, do you feel like pork chops and cheesy potatoes, hot dogs and beans, or ham sliders and chips? Man, I just realized that everything I bought is pork. This baby boy apparently wants pig. Hmm…I wonder if all this meat is going to make him a huge baby. You don't think he's going to be this giant baby just because I'm eating so much meat, do you? Ugh, that would suck. Let's hope he comes out normal-sized. You know, I've never been a huge fan of meat, but man, do I crave it now. Actually, I think I'm going to go with the pork chops because they expire sooner. That makes the most sense, don't you think?"

I don't answer Sarah because her question is rhetorical. She holds one-sided conversations like this all day long. If I wasn't in such a low place, I'd probably find them cute. But I just find it annoying. That's not fair to her, I know. She's just trying to help by filling the space with conversation. Though, to me, silence would be preferable.

Sarah continues to prattle on while I assume she starts making the pork chops when there's another knock at the door.

"I'll get it," she calls, walking through the living room and toward the front door.

She's outside for a couple of minutes before she comes back in and walks over to the couch. "It's London."

I suck in a gulp of air at the sound of her name.

"I told her that you didn't want to see her, but she's insisting on seeing you," Sarah informs me.

Shit.

"I can't." I slowly shake my head, my mouth agape.

"No problem. I'll take care of it," Sarah says cheerfully. She walks back toward the front foyer.

God, I'm such an asshole. A complete jerk.

I'm not quite sure what it is that I'm so afraid of when it comes to London, but I have this powerful feeling that I would crumble if I saw her.

London and I can never work. I'm broken, nowhere near the man that a girl like London wants. I'm mentally not capable of being a *boyfriend* to anyone at the moment.

I'd be lying if I didn't admit that a part of me, deep down, thinks she would take one look at my tattered body and run. I tell myself that it wouldn't matter if she did. She'd be doing me a favor.

Yet a bigger part thinks she wouldn't care and would love me anyway.

Oddly, that's the scariest part.

I know I would disappoint her, and I wouldn't be able to stand another failure.

I know that the right thing to do is to break up with her face-to-face. But I'm not prepared for the full-blown devastation that would hit my heart if I saw London again. I'm self-aware enough to know that I'm hanging on by a thread. A London sighting would snap the thin fiber holding me together, and I would crumble. There's only so far one can fall before they can never get up again.

Yeah, I'm a coward. An asshole. A jerk. A deplorable human being.

But I'm here, and I'm alive. For now, that's going to have to be enough.

My thoughts are silenced by Sarah's return.

She stands above me. "Well, she's gone, and I think she got the picture."

"You weren't mean to her, were you?"

Sarah looks appalled. "No, of course not."

"Okay, good." I exhale a shaky sigh of relief. Along with the air from my lungs, some of the tension escapes me.

"Great. I'm going to go finish dinner," Sarah says before walking around the couch to head back into the kitchen.

London's gone.

That thought is as equally depressing as it is satisfying, but truthfully, all I can feel is relief.

SIX

London

"Love is everything. It's the only thing."
—*London Wright*

"You're hurting me."

Loïc's words have been echoing through my mind since his pained voice uttered them over the phone two weeks ago.

How was I hurting him when all I wanted to do was love him, help him, and simply be there?

It doesn't make sense. Any of it.

I've had to stop myself from driving to his place every day. It's been so hard, too. Staying away from Loïc when he's so close has been the most difficult thing I've ever done.

I crave him. Desire him. Need him. More than anything in my life.

My body vibrates with an unsettling urge to go to him, so much so that it's physically painful.

Paige and I gave up sugar for a week a couple of years back. I can't remember why exactly. We must have been on some new health kick. Anyway, all I remember is how hard it was to kick sugar. I never realized that sugar is an addiction. When a body is used to having it and it doesn't get it, you go through withdrawal symptoms, as if you were coming off a drug. I recall, on day three of our sugar detox, we literally opened all the candy in the house, threw it in the garbage, and dumped a can of condensed cream of chicken soup on the pile of sweet goodness, so we wouldn't be tempted to dig it out of the garbage and eat it later. That's how bad it was.

Detoxing from Loïc feels the same way but ten times worse. So, I've completely disregarded my hygiene. I only shower when my hair becomes so oily that my scalp itches or my stink becomes too great, whichever one comes first. I'm a mess, ensuring that I won't succumb to a moment of weakness and drive to Loïc's to beg him to come back to me. Let's face it; if I had any chance of getting him back, it wouldn't be as this pile of grease.

Yet, the thing is, I don't have a chance of getting Loïc back. He doesn't want me. He doesn't want us. I can't for the life of me figure out why, but he doesn't.

I suppose that's what's making this all so difficult—I can't understand it. A voice in my head tells me there's something more...something I'm missing. Yes, Loïc went through a traumatic experience. Yes, he's heartbroken over Cooper. But shouldn't he need me more because of those things? Wouldn't our love make all that better?

Who knows? Maybe this is what it feels like to be the one who has been broken up with. I've never been in this position before.

But I don't believe that either. What Loïc and I had was real, and nothing can convince me otherwise. I thought I was going to marry him. We were going to have beautiful babies, raise our family, laugh, love, and be happy. We were going to grow old together, our love never wavering.

But that dream's gone.

When he begged me to let him go, I had to.

Every fiber in my being tells me that it's the wrong thing to do, but I love and respect Loïc too much to cause him pain.

Apparently, I'm not the one for him, and though I don't understand it, I have to respect it.

It's just so hard.

How long will this last?

How long will I have to feel this way? Empty, sad...devastated.

I stare at the blank white page on my laptop as the small vertical line blinks back at me, taunting me, a constant reminder of my failures.

I'm going to lose my job if I miss another deadline, but the words won't come. I've been staring at this screen all day, but all I see is Loïc. And all I feel is heartache.

I'm failing at life.

"Ugh!" I let out a groan of annoyance as I lean my head against the back of the chair and stare up at the ceiling.

"That bad?" Paige questions from my bedroom doorway.

I didn't hear her come home from work.

"It's worse," I sigh.

"Is it worse than your hair? I'm pretty sure, if we wring the grease out of that mop, we could fry up some chicken."

"Ew, that's gross, Paige."

"So is your hair, my love. So is your hair."

49

"I know. It's starting to really itch." I make a face, scrunching up my nose, to which Paige starts laughing.

"London, please go shower. It's time." Paige swipes her hand through the air, gesturing toward my bathroom.

"Fine. I can barely stand my own filth. But you can't let me go over to Loïc's tonight. Promise?"

"Promise." Paige makes a cross over her heart.

Sitting across the booth from Paige at our favorite Mexican restaurant, I'm freshly showered with a mango margarita in my hand, and I feel almost human again. It helps that the margarita glass is larger than my head.

"So, what are we going to do to get you out of this funk?" Paige asks.

"Convince Loïc to take me back," I answer with a coy voice.

"Besides that." She playfully rolls her eyes. "It's been two weeks since he called. I know it hurts. It totally sucks. But you have to move on."

"I know," I state as I twirl the straw around in my glass. "I'm trying."

"Maybe you just need a change of scenery. We should fly to Cali this weekend and hang out with Georgia. Your sister can cheer anyone up."

Shrugging, I agree, "Yeah, that could be fun."

"Well, we have to do something. We can't have you moping around forever. Babe, I know this isn't what you wanted, but there are two people in a relationship. You have to respect what Loïc wants."

"Obviously, I know that." I let out a sigh.

"So, after dinner, we'll call Georgia and set up a girls' weekend. It will be a blast," Paige says with a smile as she raises her hefty margarita glass. "A toast." She beams.

I can't help but smile back. She's such a great friend.

I raise my now mostly empty glass and tilt it in to tap hers. "To moving on and being happy."

Paige continues, "To realizing that we only have one life to live and to live it to the fullest."

I start to say, *Cheers*, but Paige keeps talking in the never-ending toast, "To friendship and new experiences. And *c'est la vie*."

I wait hesitantly, expecting more to come.

"Cheers!" Paige clinks her glass against mine.

"Cheers!" I drink down the rest of my mango drink. Dropping my glass from my lips, I say with a tilt of my head, "Are you seriously using sayings from other languages as advice now?"

"It's a universal saying, and at least this one applies to the situation."

"Are you sure?" I throw Paige a smirk, the corner of my lips turning up into a grin.

"Yeah, I think so." Paige's eyebrows furrow in the center, like they always do when she's deep in thought. "Doesn't it mean, like, *seize the day*?"

"It means, *that's life*." I shake my head with a laugh.

"Whatever. It still applies." She tosses a chip in her mouth. "Hey, did you call Maggie today?"

"Yeah, I did…this morning." I raise my empty margarita glass toward the waiter who's across the room.

With a smile, he mouths, *One more?*

I nod. I hardly need a second one of these bad boys, but the feeling is so much more preferable to the deep-seated misery that's been saturating my mind as of late.

"And?" Paige asks, snapping me out of my thoughts.

"Oh, well…it was weird," I admit.

"Why?"

"Well…" I think back to the awkward conversation that I had with Maggie earlier. "It wasn't a natural talk. It felt forced."

"Really?"

I nod. "Yeah, it's almost like Maggie feels torn between Loïc and me, and she has more history with Loïc. Plus, you know…Cooper and Loïc were so close. So, for that fact alone, I figure, if she has to choose sides, she'll choose Loïc. I got the feeling that she felt guilty for talking to me, like she was abusing Loïc's trust or something."

"Did she say anything about Loïc? Has she talked to him about you?"

"She said that she's seen him recently, and he looks tired but okay. She said that she brought me up, but he quickly shut her down, stating that he didn't want to talk about me. So, she didn't bring me up again."

"Ouch." Paige makes a face.

"I know." I roll my eyes. "Not good."

"Well"—Paige lets out a large sigh—"it's not surprising though either."

I look down to my half-eaten burrito. "I know, but it still hurts."

"I'm sorry."

I frown, raising my shoulders and letting them fall. "It is what it is," I say without conviction.

"Señorita!" Our server places another giant glass in front of me. "You look like you need this."

"Oh, I do, José. Thank you so much." I start drinking the cold mango-flavored goodness before José turns to leave.

As I finish my drink, Paige catches me up on her life, which basically consists of work. I'm so proud of my best friend. She has gotten several promotions at her job since she's been there. We've both changed so much in this past year. Last May, our biggest worry was what color nail polish we were going to choose for our mani-pedis.

And, now…

I glance down to my phone and take in the date. I will never forget this date for as long as I live. A year ago today, I was rubbing my bikini-clad body all over a dirty truck in hopes of gaining the attention of a beautiful boy with eyes like the ocean.

And, now…

I feel like I'm drowning in that ocean, unable to escape his depths.

"Paige, can we go?" I say abruptly, interrupting her latest story.

"Um, sure." She reaches for her purse and pulls out her car keys. "Go wait in the car. I'll pay the bill and be out, okay?"

I nod. "Okay. Thank you."

I bolt out of the booth and head toward the exit. Sometimes, when I'm thinking about Loïc, it all becomes too much, and I physically can't breathe. It feels like the walls are closing in on me, and I'm suffocating. I hate it. I despise my inability to stop it, but when it hits…it just decimates me.

I lean against Paige's car. The warm spring wind feels good against my skin. The tears come, streaming down my face. I am powerless to stop them.

When the pain becomes too much to bear, the crying ensues. It's a part of my life now. To be honest, it feels good to cry. It sounds silly, but sometimes, I feel like the tears carry some of the anguish away. It's my body's self-preservation technique.

It just hurts so much. Every second of every day, it hurts.

I miss him, and truthfully, I don't know where to go from here. I hardly know who I am anymore. I'm certainly no longer the girl I was a year ago, before I met Loïc. When one has experienced what it means to love someone with everything they are, they can no longer go back to who they were before.

Since I've experienced true, real, unadulterated love, the things that used to give my life meaning seem insignificant now. I've come to realize how shallow my life truly was. On the outside, I'm sure I looked like a girl who had it all. At the time, I thought I did, too. All of it was just a facade though.

The reality is, love is everything. It's the only thing.

Without it, I'm simply empty. It's the loneliest feeling in the world.

I realize that I'm not the only person who's ever gone through heartache. I know that people move on from it all the time. I just don't know how.

Yet…there's a voice. It's small and quiet, but it's there. And it's telling me that I need a change. I can't expect to feel whole, to be happy again, if I continue doing what I'm currently doing.

Loïc has been in Michigan for several weeks. It's been a solid two weeks since that fateful phone call, yet I'm standing here, in the midst of my grief, the same as I've been since he told me to let him go. Nothing is changing, and I have a feeling it won't until I do.

Paige's face falls when she sees my tear-stained cheeks. "Oh, London." She pulls me into a hug.

I hold her tight, allowing her unconditional love to fold me in its warmth for a moment.

After a few breaths, I pull back. "Can we drive past his house? Please?"

"London," Paige protests, carrying a tone of warning.

"I know, but I just *need* to. *Please*. We won't stop. We're in your car, so even if he's outside, he probably won't notice. I need to…just this once. I realize it's probably not going to help anything, but I feel like I have to see a part of him, even his house, one more time." I tightly grasp Paige's arms.

She sighs loudly, and I know I've won.

"Okay, but just this one time," she says like a scolding parent.

"Thank you." I smile.

"Get in the car," she states with zero enthusiasm.

When we're both buckled up, Paige pulls out of the parking lot and heads in the direction of Loïc's house. "I can't believe I agreed to this."

"Thank you," I say again sweetly.

"If he's out in the yard or something, you'd better not jump out of my moving car, or I will never talk to you again."

"Yes, you will."

She shakes her head. "Well, I won't be able to if you're dead."

"I'm not going to jump out of your car." I grin, feeling suddenly lighter with the prospect of possibly seeing Loïc through his window—or better yet, in his yard, on the horizon. God, I sound like a stalker, but I'm okay with that.

The closer we get to Loïc's neighborhood, the faster my heart beats. I wipe my sweaty palms on my shorts as Paige turns onto his street.

"Okay, drive by really slow!" I shout.

"I will. Calm down." Paige chuckles.

My eyes start to search frantically before his house comes into view. I'm dying to get a glimpse of Loïc, and I know it's juvenile and bordering on crazy, but I just miss him so much.

When his house is visible, I see a person walking up to his front porch. My body shudders with grief because it's not him. It's *her*.

As Paige passes his house, I don't get a glimpse of the love of my life; instead, I see the pregnant hooker he's living with. Sarah is walking toward the house, away from the car in the drive that I'm assuming is hers. She's wearing short jean shorts and a white tank top. The mounds of her front are clearly visible, all three of them—her boobs and giant belly. And I hate her more because she still looks hot, even with the belly.

Worst of all, she's carrying light-violet plastic bags, ones that I would recognize anywhere because they are the take-out bags from my favorite Thai restaurant. It's the one that opened up right after Loïc left. I told him all about it in my letters to him while he was in Afghanistan. I told him how much I loved it and how I couldn't wait to take him there. But, now, she's bringing it to him. She's bringing *my* Thai from *my* restaurant to *my* Loïc.

I hate her. So much.

I understand that the source of my anger isn't really her, but it's the fact that Loïc no longer wants me.

But, though I've considered it, I could never hate Loïc. I love him too damn much, so I'm going to hate her. And, oh, I do.

As the house, the hooker, and the violet take-out bags get smaller behind me in the distance, all I feel is complete and utter despair.

My shoulders begin to shake as the sobs violently work their way out of me. Hot tears stream down my face like rivers because the sadness is simply too much to contain.

SEVEN

London

> *"Heartbreak is the most painful kind of torture,*
> *and the mind is its greatest ally."*
> —London Wright

I've had the Notes app on my phone open for what seems like hours now, specifically the entry from New Year's Eve of last year.

"Oh, Brad. Brad, Brad, Brad, Brad, Brad..." I say with a sigh.

I continue to repeat his name.

Why? I'm not so sure. And, the more I say it, the weirder it sounds.

"Brad." I nod.

"Brad." My tone is higher.

"*Braaad*," I say, drawing out his name.

It's official. I've up and gone crazy.

I've been contemplating calling him all day—truthfully, the better part of this past week. Yet I haven't been able to bring myself to do it.

It's been one week since Paige and I stalked past Loïc's house and saw *her* walking into the house with the offending bags of Thai food.

Instead of spending last weekend in California with my best friend and sister, like Paige and I had planned last week at dinner, I spent it alone in my room, wallowing in my self-pity and torturing myself by looking at pictures of Loïc and me on my phone.

I hate who I've become. This isn't me, and it's infuriating. I've never let a boy dictate my self-worth or my happiness. Then again, I've never been in love before, and Loïc isn't just any boy. He's a man.

The man for me, a small voice echoes in my mind.

Oh, stop it!

I loathe myself right now. I don't understand why I can't break out of this funk. But I know I need to. This isn't healthy for me. It's not who I am. I'm so much stronger than this. I've just seemed to misplace my backbone at the moment.

Paige's words from last week have been on a continuous loop in my mind. *"Maybe you just need a change of scenery."*

I think she's right. Everywhere I look, I'm surrounded by reminders of my time with Loïc, and it's painful. It's crazy to think that I've spent five years in this city, yet everything brings back images of only the past year. Long gone are the fond recollections of my time in college. As I go through my day, all I see is Loïc, Loïc, Loïc.

I can't do it anymore. Maybe that means I'm not the strong woman I thought I was. I'm not sure. But I simply can't continue like this. I'm fading. No matter what I do or what I say, I can't move on. Thoughts of Loïc consume me, and it has to stop.

Heartbreak is the most painful kind of torture, and the mind is its greatest ally.

I can't stop thinking about Loïc and how much I love him. The hows, the whys, and the explanations that might never come plague my brain with sorrow. The what-ifs are a constant torment. I might never know what went through Loïc's mind to make him want to end our relationship, and not knowing is the hardest part.

Yet none of that matters. I can't control another person. I get that. I can't make Loïc give me an explanation. I can't make him change his mind and force him to love me again.

I can only control my own choices, and right now, I'm failing miserably.

So, yes…perhaps I do need a change of scenery. And not just for a weekend. It's going to have to be for much longer.

I don't want to leave Paige. I'll miss her like crazy, but I know that, no matter where our lives lead us, we'll always be the best of friends. Paige is my family, and distance won't change that.

And that is why I'm staring at Brad's contact information. Brad Abernathy, senior editor of the *Los Angeles Times*. Let's face it; Brad only offered me a job because he wanted to get in my pants. I know this. I've been writing articles for a local online news outlet. That's hardly the *LA Times*. But I'd also be stupid not to consider a position there, regardless of why I was being offered it. That is…if the offer is still on the table. It was six months ago. Just because Brad was attracted to me and could use his connections to offer me my dream job doesn't mean that I owe him anything.

Here goes nothing.

I let out a sigh, full of nerves, as his number starts to ring. I'm hoping it goes to voice mail. It's much easier to feign confidence over voice mail.

But I'm not that lucky.

"Hello?" he answers, his voice full of poise and swagger, just like I remember.

"Hi, Brad?" The greeting comes out more as a question.

"Yes?"

I clear my throat. "Hi. I don't know if you remember me, but we met on New Year's Eve last year. You put your information into my phone."

"London?" he questions.

My name coming over the phone startles me. For some reason, I was convinced that he wouldn't remember me. It's been half of a year since I ran out of that club, and honestly, it feels like a lifetime ago.

"Yeah. London Wright. I'm surprised you remembered my name."

"Of course I do. It's not everyday that I meet someone as memorable as you." His deep voice is thick with sexual undertones, or maybe I'm just reading too much into it, and he always sounds like that.

"Oh…well, I know it's been a while, but I was thinking about relocating to LA. I wondered if the position we spoke about was still available and if there was a chance that I might be able to get an interview." Goodness, I sound like a rambling idiot. *Get your crap together, London.*

"No"—he chuckles—"that position has been filled for a while now."

"Right. Of course."

I don't know what I was expecting. Of course it's been filled. It was silly to get my hopes up, even for a minute.

"I'm sure I could find an open position around here for you," he says, his voice smooth.

What?

"Really?" I ask in disbelief.

"I'll look around. Something's bound to open up. When were you thinking about moving out this way?"

"Honestly, as soon as I can. I just need a job first."

"I'll tell you what. I left my email in your phone, correct?"

"Yeah, you did."

"Great. Then, why don't you send me your résumé and cover letter. I'll find a position for you and start everything with HR. Then, we'll send over our offer and paperwork for you to sign sometime tomorrow."

I can't believe my luck, but it isn't adding up. "What about the interview process? Don't I need to go through that?"

"We'll consider this a phone interview. I think you're going to fit in well here."

I hear the smile in his voice.

This isn't typically how things work, but I don't have it in me to care right now. *I'm going to be writing for the LA Times!* More importantly, I'm going to be living far away from Michigan where my heart will hopefully finally be able to heal.

"That's amazing. Thank you so much, Brad—um, Mr. Abernathy?"

The rich timbre of his laugh sounds through the earpiece of my phone.

"Brad, London. Definitely Brad."

"Okay. Well, thank you so much, Brad. I can't tell you how much this job means to me. I will do my very best for your paper."

"I know you will. Get that information sent over to me, and we'll get the ball rolling."

"I will." A genuine smile crosses my face for the first time in months.

"We'll talk soon. Good-bye, London."

"Good-bye."

The line goes dead. I hold the phone to my chest and fall to my bed with a giddy laugh. *I'm going to be writing for the freaking Los Angeles Times! I can't believe this.*

I jump onto my feet and begin to bounce atop my mattress. For a brief moment, I allow myself to only think about LA and this fantastic job opportunity. I continue to jump on my bed, like a little kid, letting out squeals of celebration, and for the first time in a very long while, I feel human again. I have a purpose.

Amid my jovial merriment, Paige opens my door, just coming home from work. She doesn't even ask what's going on. She simply kicks off her heels and leaps onto my bed. Grabbing my hands, she starts jumping with me. Her face is aglow with a giant smile as she revels in happiness for me.

She is such a gift. Like a true friend, she doesn't need to know the reasons to support me. She's just there.

After another minute of springing atop my mattress, we plop down onto my bed, breathing heavily from our celebration. The second my head hits my pillow and my body stills, the tears begin to fall. In an instant, I'm a sobbing mess.

I sit up, and Paige pulls me into a hug. The weight of my current situation pulls on my heart.

I'm leaving.

I'm leaving Paige.
I'm leaving Michigan.
I'm leaving Loïc.

The last thought hurts the most because I know that I will have to officially close the chapter on Loïc and our relationship. Moving across the country will be the force I need to turn the page to the next chapter, even when I hoped the last one would have turned into another book. Just because my story with Loïc is over doesn't mean the novel of my life is. I have a lot more to tell, and I'm hoping this job will give me the courage to do so.

"I have some news," I say, pulling away from Paige's embrace.

"Okay..." Paige nods in encouragement.

"Well, remember that guy we met on New Year's Eve, the one who works for the *LA Times*?"

"Yeah."

"Well, I called him, and he offered me a job in California."

Tears begin to stream down Paige's cheeks as she says, "I'm so happy for you!"

When she pulls me into another hug, I say, "I'm sorry."

"Oh, don't be, London. I get it. I'm going to miss you like crazy, but I think this is going to be really good for you. I know you're not happy here."

I marginally lean back so that I'm facing her. "I just didn't know what else to do." I shrug.

"I know." She nods. "This is great, London. Really. I mean, the *LA Times*! That's amazing! Plus, you'll get a fresh start, which I think you need. Sure, we won't see each other every day, but you'll always be my best friend. That will never change."

"Exactly. Plus, we'll visit and text and talk all the time."

"Totally," Paige agrees. "I mean, we can't be roommates forever. That's life."

"Right." I nod.

"You know what they say..." Paige's face lights up.

"What's that?" I ask on a sigh, knowing she's about to make zero sense.

She lets out an exhale. *"Make sure to put all your eggs in one basket."* She beams with positivity.

I furrow my brows before responding, "Isn't it supposed to be, *Don't put all your eggs in one basket?*"

"But you're putting all your eggs in one basket with this LA thing. Why would I say not to?" Paige tilts her head to the side in question.

"I don't know, but that's the way the saying goes. You're *not* supposed to put all your eggs in one basket because you're supposed to leave yourself with different options, you know? Hence, the saying. But I *am* putting all my eggs in one basket because I'm relying on this LA job to come through. So, the saying doesn't make sense."

"Right. That's why I said to put them all in one basket." Paige widens her eyes, as if to say, *Duh.*

"But that's not the saying, Paige. You're not supposed to put all your eggs in one basket," I say, exasperated.

"Why are you so stuck on this egg thing? You don't even like eggs that much." Paige scrunches her lips together.

"OMG! You brought this entire thing up!" I scoff before breaking out in laughter. Wrapping my arms around Paige, I pull her into a hug. "I'm going to miss you so much."

"Me, too." She squeezes me back. *"A bird in the hand is worth two in the bush,* right?"

"You're ridiculous." I chuckle. "I'm not even going there."

She pulls back and looks me in the eyes. "What are you going to do without all my words of advice?"

"Be a hell of a lot less confused!" I smile big. "Though I have a feeling I'm going to be getting it anyway. You're going to be blowing up my phone."

"Just as much as you'll be blowing up mine."

"You know it." I grin. "I love you, Paigey Poo."

"I love you, London."

It's surreal to think that I'm going to be moving across the country, but I have a really good feeling about it.

I don't know if I'll ever live in Michigan again. I kind of doubt it.

But I'm hoping, with time and distance, eventually, when I think back to my time in this state, I'll remember all the great experiences I had in college and my memories with Paige. This home has given me so much more than heartbreak. Someday, my heart will be healed enough to remember that.

EIGHT

Loïc

"My life is a daily battle of fighting
to simply exist."
—Loïc Berkeley

"I just don't know what to name him. You have to give me suggestions, Loïc," Sarah whines beside me.

She's lying atop a blanket on the grass in a black string bikini. I can just see her closed eyelids behind the sunglasses as her face points up toward the midday sun.

Sitting in a lounge chair beside her, I'm trying to soak up the vitamin D that she is so adamant about. She says that the sun always makes people feel better. I decided to humor her since, for June, the humidity and heat aren't excessive today and because I could use some non-couch time.

I pull in slow, steady breaths as the rays of the sun heat my skin. Truthfully, I could stand to feel better—to feel anything actually. I've been back for over a month, and I'm still waiting for something, anything, to happen that will allow me to feel human again. My life is just...void. It's lacking purpose, feelings, desire...basically everything. I'm merely existing, and I don't know what to do to make it better.

"Loïc!" Sarah shrieks, breaking my attempt at peaceful meditation. "Did you hear me?"

"I've told you"—I carefully measure my voice, making sure the tone carries a semblance of compassion—"it is totally your call, Sarah. Your baby, your choice."

"But you're going to be a big part in his life. I want you to be involved. I want you to care."

I let out a sigh. "I do care."

"I know you do. I wish you showed it a little more."

"I'm doing the best I can, Sarah."

I admit, sometimes, I wish she would just go and leave me to wallow on my couch alone. But I realize that it's better that she's here. It's important that I'm accountable to someone. I'm afraid I'd lose myself completely if I weren't.

"I know you are. I'm sorry, Loïc. I'm more sensitive now—you know, the hormones and all." Her voice picks up an octave. "So, what about Henry, after your granddad? Or William, after your dad? Do you like either of those names?"

"Any name is fine. Name him what you like. You don't have to name him after my family. It doesn't matter."

Her whine returns as she says, "It matters to me, Loïc. We're naming a human here. It is a big deal."

"What about that baby name book that you bought the other day? You should read through it and make a list of names you like," I suggest.

"Oh, good idea! So, I'll make a list of names, and then I'll read them off to you, so we can decide together."

"Okay," I concede.

"Great!" She hops off the blanket faster than a pregnant woman should be able to and rushes into the house.

Sarah has been hunched over the kitchen table all afternoon, studying that baby name book like a college student preparing for final exams. From the living room couch, I've heard her frantically write names, cross them off, and flip pages, like a woman on a mission.

The doorbell rings.

"I got it!" Sarah calls, as she does every time even though I've never attempted to get the door since she's been here.

After a few minutes, she walks by with a large pizza box. I inhale the aroma of melted cheese, buttery garlic, and pepperoni as she passes behind the couch. I reach for my crutches. Positioning them beneath my arms, I use them to pull myself off the couch. I take a moment to balance on my one foot before using the crutches to assist me to the kitchen.

Most days, I try to wear my prosthetic leg, but others, I simply need a break from it. I know I'll eventually get used to it, but for now, it's an annoyance. It brings an uncomfortable, hot, itchy, unnatural presence to my daily life, contributing to my slow decline toward insanity.

Sarah sets the table for two. She places a glass of ice water in front of me as I take the first bite of my pizza slice.

"So, I've finally narrowed down the list to my top name choices," Sarah says excitedly.

"Good. You've been working hard on that list."

"I know. I've gone back and forth through the boy names more times than I can count. But I finally have a concise list. Now, I just need you to help me choose."

"All right, let's hear them."

"Okay!" She reaches back to the counter to grab the piece of paper that she's been writing on and pushes her plate to the side. "Remember, this is my final list. So, any of these names would work. I really want your opinion."

I force a smile. "I'm ready."

"So, of course, we still have Henry and William on the table. Then, I also like Wyatt, Grant, Evan, Andrew, Jax, Stephen, Jacob, Roman, Evan—oh, wait, I already said Evan. I must really like that one if I wrote it twice." She laughs to herself. "Then, I have Kline, Luca, Gunnar, Xander, Reese, Lawson, Kyler, Trystan, Creed, Kace, Grey, Rowan, Garrett, Dax, Bowie, Beckett, Kale, Jace, and Chandler." She stops and pulls in a breath.

"Oh, wow—" I start to say.

She halts the rest of my thought. "Wait, I'm not done. I also like Kyler—oops, said that. So, we also have Lucas, Grayson, Mitchell, Logan, Madden, Landon, Sullivan, Jameson, Fordson, Zachary, Broderick, Corban, Roan, Hendrix, Ryan, Camden, Raine, Asten, Asher, Carter, Brody, Jagger, Kingston, Kohl, Ramsey, Reaves, Rhys, Saxton, Noah, Cooper, Eli, Elijah, Dean, Samuel, Connor, Braeden, Thad, Brant, Colby, Crosby, Garth, Ivan, Coulter, Kelby, Kirk, Fitz, Jameson, Knox, Langdon, Paxton, Prescott, Smith, Stone, Teague, Vaughn, and Walker."

I wait, expecting more name diarrhea to explode from her mouth.

But, instead of saying another name, she expectantly looks at me. "So?"

"Holy hell, Sarah. That's your final list?"

"Yeah," she answers innocently.

"And you don't think you could have narrowed it down at all?"

She seems offended. "I did! Like, a lot. I probably had, like, four times that at one point."

"What'd you do? Just copy down every name in the book?"

"No," she huffs. "I thought long and hard about each name and narrowed it down to my favorites."

"Well, I've got nothing for ya." I shrug.

"What do you mean?" Her eyes widen.

"I mean, I can't even remember one name you said because you were rattling them off faster than I could take them in."

"I'll read them again." She lowers her face to the paper.

"No. Please don't." I hold up my hand. "Let me know when you've narrowed it down a little more, like when your list totals two or three."

"That's, like, impossible!"

I place my hand on Sarah's. "Calm down. You have time. You've accomplished much harder things in your life than picking a name. It'll be okay."

"But this is the most important thing I've ever done, Loïc. I've failed at everything. I can't fail at this." Her voice falters as her eyes fill with tears.

"Sarah…" I start to say.

"No, seriously…" A tear falls down her cheek. "We had the shittiest of childhoods, Loïc. I want my baby to have the best. I've already failed by not doing it the right

73

way and giving him a father. He needs a strong name. It has to be perfect."

"Hey"—I lean in and pull her into a hug—"listen to me. There is no such thing as perfect, Sarah. Your life will have more ups and downs, and that's okay. The main thing that children need is love, and you'll make sure he feels loved. Everything else will work itself out."

I lean back so that I can look into her big blue eyes. "Whichever name you choose will be the right one because you chose it, his mother, who loves him more than anything in the world. Okay?"

"Okay." She nods, unsure.

"You're going to rock this motherhood thing. Just wait." I shoot her a wink before I sit back in my chair and grab another slice of pizza.

"I'm glad you have confidence in me."

"I do." I smile.

Sarah and I finish up eating. After tidying up the kitchen, we plop down on the couch to watch a movie. Sarah holds two Blu-ray cases in her hand.

"I picked up two movies from Redbox that I thought you would like—*Batman Versus Superman* or *Deadpool*. You choose."

My chest constricts with pain the second she says *Deadpool*. Memories of repeatedly watching the movie while on deployment surface. Anything that reminds me of deployment automatically reminds me of Cooper. I will never be able to separate the two.

I let out a rush of air. "*Batman*," I hastily spit out, wiping my sweaty palms against my shorts.

Sarah appears concerned and opens her mouth to speak before clamping it shut and simply nodding. She occupies herself by setting up the movie, taking longer than usual. I use the bonus time to get my shit together.

Once I start spiraling down with Cooper regrets, it's difficult to bring myself back to the present.

My therapists, both in Germany and in DC, taught me many strategies to stop the panic attacks. I quickly run through them—counting, staying in the moment, breathing, and acknowledging my fear. After a tense moment, my heart rate begins to slow, and I can inhale without the overwhelming tightness of my chest interfering. Honestly, I don't think it's any of the specific techniques as much as the concentration I use to remember the different strategies. It takes my mind off the trigger long enough for me to regain control.

Sarah sits next to me as the movie starts. This movie is completely up my alley. I love any Marvel or DC Comics movies. As a teen, I was able to get my hands on a few comic books. They were light enough and took up such little space that I was able to carry them with me as Sarah and I made our trek from Texas to Arizona. They were my only reading material for a couple of years, and I read those comics many times over.

Yet, as I sit here, I'm finding it difficult to even focus on the movie at all. We've been watching it for at least an hour, and I can't even say what it is about.

Sarah reaches for the remote and pauses the movie. "I don't know if I'm in the mood for this one tonight. We can watch it another time."

"Yeah, I agree."

I know she's just trying to make me happy, sensing my energy. But, even if I insisted she finish watching it, I know she wouldn't. Sarah has always been able to read me, and she's as loyal as they come.

"Let's just relax." She sighs, leaning into my side.

"Okay." I situate myself so that I'm lying back on the couch.

Sarah follows me down, her belly facing the side, as she lays her head on my bare stomach.

The two of us just lie like this in silence for a long time. It's probably the best time I've had with Sarah since we've been living together. That's a sad truth to admit, but it's my reality.

I'm starting to drift off to sleep when I feel her hand start to glide across my abdomen.

Sarah and I have always been close. When we were homeless, we slept together almost every night, our limbs entangled as we clung to each other for warmth and comfort. Yet there is something different about the way she's touching me now. It's more intimate somehow.

My muscles tighten in response as her caress, loving and determined, teases its way over my skin. Her fingertip traces shapes on my body with minimal pressure. Her touch is almost a whisper. If I wasn't paying attention, I might not even feel it, but I do. It resonates within, like a shout, and my mind screams with unrest.

I swallow and pull in a stream of air. "Sarah?"

"Shh…it's okay, Loïc," she murmurs. Her warm breath assaults my skin.

Then, I feel it—her soft lips gently kissing up my chest.

Squeezing my eyes closed, I try to make sense of it all, but I don't have any success. The truth is, nothing in my life has significant meaning anymore. I wish I could feel love again, but there's no room for such a luxury.

My life is a daily battle of fighting to simply exist. I fight to get up every morning, to breathe, to eat, to function. It's an exhausting daily ritual just to make it to nighttime when I can close my eyes and drift off into oblivion.

And then I wake up to do it all again.

Every day.

Being in this position with anyone isn't a possibility right now.

But, with Sarah, it'll never be an option.

She's moving up my body. She kisses my neck.

"Sarah, stop."

"Just let me love you," she whispers.

"You know you don't have to do that. We've been through this before." I sigh, thinking about all the times similar scenarios happened between Sarah and me when we were younger.

"It's not like that, Loïc." She lifts herself up onto her elbows, resting her forearms against my chest, and peers into my eyes. "This isn't me as a broken girl, desperately trying to feel love. This is me as an adult, telling you that I love you. I want a life with you, Loïc. There is no one that can love you like I can, and there is no one who has ever loved me as much as you have. We're meant to be together."

"You're my family," I respond. "Of course I love you. I would do anything to help you, to make you happy. But I don't love you like that."

She gives her head a slight shake. "You don't think you love me in that way because you've always treated me like a sister, but if you give it a chance, I know it can work between us. We can be together, raise this little boy, and be a real family. You don't have to be Uncle Loïc. You can be Daddy."

"I can't."

"I know," she sighs, a trace of sorrow lining her voice. "I know that things are rough for you right now, but"—her demeanor changes as a smile graces her face— "that actually makes this more perfect because this baby and I can make you happy. We will love you so much that your heart will heal. You and I came into each other's lives for a reason. We are meant to be together. Just please think about it."

"I don't believe that everything happens for a reason, Sarah. Fate and destiny and all that shit aren't real." I push up against the couch cushions until I'm sitting up.

Sarah sits beside me, turning to face me. She stares at me for a moment. "You are my destiny, Loïc. You came into my life like a knight in shining armor and rescued me from a life of hell. You saved me. That's fate. I have loved you ever since you grabbed my hand and we ran out of that house when I was thirteen."

I've always hated the idea of fate. For a brief moment, when I was with London and life was so great and I felt true happiness, I thought, *Maybe?*

But then it all came crashing down again, like it always does, reminding me that nothing happens for a reason.

My temper flares beneath the surface, and I will it to stay contained as I speak, "Sarah, to say that everything happens for a reason is to say that my parents were supposed to die and my grandparents were destined to abandon me. It's to say that you were supposed to be molested, raped, and left by all those who were supposed to love you the most. It's to say that Cooper—the best man I've ever known—was supposed to die. That's bullshit, Sarah. Things simply do not happen for a reason. Life has no rhyme or reason, and shitty things happen to good people every single day. Life isn't love, destiny, rainbows, and butterflies. Life is shit. It's painful and hard. It's surviving when you want to give up."

"No, Loïc…" Sarah's lip trembles as tears escape from her eyes. She places her hand on my good leg and squeezes gently. "Life gives us heartache, so we can appreciate the joy. You taught me that."

"No, I didn't."

"Not with words, but with your actions. You showed me that, even in the darkest of times, there is light to be found. You showed me that, even when you have nothing, if you have love, you have enough. You showed me that, if we persevere through the difficult times, something good will be waiting for us at the end. Yeah, life can be hard. But you showed me that, through it all, I deserve happiness. Well, guess what? You deserve the same. We've put in our dues. We've suffered. We're allowed to be happy now. Let's build a life together—you and me against the world. And I guarantee, because of all the crap that we've overcome, we'll appreciate it that much more."

"I'm sorry, Sarah. Whoever you thought I was, I can assure you, I'm not. I will love you and this baby as much as I can for as long as I'm able. But I can't give you the life you deserve. For me, life is simply existing until I die. You and this baby deserve a happy life." I reach for my crutches and stand.

She stands with me, disappointment gleaming in her eyes. "And you don't? Loïc, I want to help you. Tell me how. How can I make you happy?"

"Just leave me alone, please," I plead as I start toward my bedroom.

From behind me, Sarah sadly calls out, "I'm not giving up on you."

I ignore her as I shut my bedroom door behind me.

NINE

London

"I miss me."
—London Wright

Looking through the front windshield as we approach Main Street in Los Angeles, my stomach does a flip as I read *THE TIMES* engraved in the stone of the building high above the tops of the palm trees lining the street.

Yes, I said, *palm trees*. Score for California.

This is so surreal.

I thank my Uber driver and hop out of his car. I stand for a moment and let my emotions settle. I'm about to walk into my dream job and my new life.

Just a week ago, I summoned the courage to call Brad about a job at the paper, and now, I'm here. One week was all it took to pack up the last five years of my life and move across the country.

Saying good-bye to Paige was so hard. We both shed many tears, but I will still see her often. My dad owns the house that we lived in, so for now, Paige will continue to stay there. I don't think he's in any rush to sell it. Plus, when I decide to visit Michigan, I'll have a place to stay.

I take a deep breath before pulling the tall glass door open and entering the building. Life goes on, as they say, and I am ready for this. I'm so ready not to hurt. I'm ready to do something I love and to feel like me again.

I miss *me*. I want the awesome London back, not the heartbroken whiny pants. Seriously, that version of myself is annoying.

As I enter, I smile when I see the large globe in the main corridor. I've only seen it in pictures. I click open my Snapchat app and take a selfie with the globe behind me. As I wait for the elevator, I quickly send the photo to everyone I care about. I post it on my story and send it to Paige, Georgia, my mom and dad, and a few of my sorority sisters. I click next to Maggie's name but unselect it just as quickly. I love Maggie, always will. But some friendships just aren't meant to last forever. Loïc got Maggie in the breakup, as he should. Our friendship has been slowly fizzling out since Loïc's return, and I've come to peace with it. It's hard to stay close with someone when there's so much we can't talk about. It's okay. I'm glad Loïc has her.

As the elevator ascends, I run my palms down my Calvin Klein pencil skirt. My last hurrah as roommates with Paige was a huge shopping spree where I bought all sorts of gorgeous professional clothing. I actually bought Paige this exact outfit as I ruined hers in a battle with marinara sauce months back.

I miss that girl.

I step out of the elevator and onto Brad's floor, and I am immediately greeted by a secretary.

"Hello. How can I help you?"

Her bright red hair, Southern accent, and huge smile take me aback a bit. She seems to be about my age, and I immediately like her even though she isn't at all what I expected.

For some reason, I was thinking the secretary would be an exact replica to the ones in the *Fifty Shades of Grey* movie. I've obviously thought a little too much about what LA would be like.

"Hi. I'm here to see Mr. Abernathy."

"Oh, you must be London!"

I nod.

"We are so excited to have ya here. Brad has told us all about you." She beams before hitting a button on her phone. "Brad, Ms. Wright's here."

I hear Brad tell her to send me in, and I can't help but wonder exactly what Brad had to tell about me. He hardly knows me.

"You can head on back. He's through those doors right there." She points to a tall set of wooden doors to the right of her desk. "I'm Kate, by the way. I'm new to California, too. I know this is totally forward and all, but I have a two-bedroom apartment and am looking for a roommate. Let me know if you need a place to stay," she says cheerfully with a wide grin.

"Okay, I will. Thank you." I smile back at her before heading toward Brad's office.

I'm currently staying at a hotel. My dad is shopping around for a nice apartment for me, but I have to admit that the thought of moving in with Kate and financially doing this whole LA thing on my own is kind of exciting.

Before I can knock on Brad's door, it swings open, and I'm met with the man I remember from New Year's Eve. He looks like a young Brad Pitt with short hair, straight from the set of *Fight Club*, and he's wearing a very expensive, sexy suit. I have no interest in anything but a professional relationship with this guy, but man, is he ever beautiful. I wouldn't have a heartbeat if I couldn't at least admit that much.

"London."

His perfect smile disarms me for a second with little unwanted butterflies doing flips in my stomach.

"Hello, Brad." I extend my hand out to his and shake firmly, ignoring the way in which his hand seems to linger in mine longer than it should.

"Come in." He motions toward the interior of his office. "Take a seat."

I sit in a dark brown leather chair that faces his large mahogany desk.

"It's so good to see you again," he says as he sits behind his desk.

"Thank you again for this opportunity, Brad. I'm so excited to work here."

"Of course. So, you know that you're going to be writing for the *LA Now* section, so you could be covering anything from local festivals to cheating celebrities to abnormal weather to shootings." He chuckles. "You'll get the full LA experience."

"Okay." I nod.

"So, how about I show you around? Let you see your office, and then we'll head out to dinner to celebrate."

"I have an office?" The tone of my voice rises an octave.

He shrugs. "It's probably more of a cubical, but office sounds better."

"Hey, a cubical works for me." I grin.

I'm full from an incredible dinner and happy to be in good company. Brad really is a cool guy, and I can tell he'll be a great boss. I was nervous going into this dinner, but it's going great. The wine helps.

Speaking of amazing wine, I take another sip of the delicious red. I don't remember what Brad said it was called, but it's smooth and rich, and it goes down entirely too quickly.

"So, tell me, Mr. Brad Abernathy. Do you take all your new employees out to extravagant dinners?" I ask. The wine has apparently reached the point where I've stopped filtering my thoughts, and I'm allowing them all to just escape.

"Not all of them," Brad replies with a slight smirk.

Feeling my cheeks flush, I place my wine glass down on the table. No matter how much it beckons me, I will not finish my fourth glass because then Brad would pour me a fifth, and that would present all sorts of problems.

"Which ones then?"

"Ones that I have an interest in spending time with," he answers simply.

"You know I'm not going to sleep with you," my wine brain makes me say. I press my lips together and raise my eyebrows in warning.

"You know I didn't ask you to," Brad responds easily.

"All right, just wanted to get that out there." I nod with an air of smugness.

"So, tell me, how do you like LA so far?"

"I haven't seen or done much yet. My flight got in late last night. I checked into the hotel and came to see you today. That's pretty much the extent of it."

"How long are you planning on staying at the hotel?"

"I'm not sure. But just until I find a place of my own."

"Kate tells me that she's going to convince you to move in with her. Has she approached you yet?"

I let out a small chuckle. "Yes, actually...like thirty seconds after I met her."

"And?" he prompts with a hint of amusement lining his voice.

"I don't know. I hardly know her, of course, but she seems really fun. I suppose it's an option for now. Eventually, I want to do the whole independent thing. You know, first great job deserves my first place on my own. I'll think about it. It might be nice to have someone to talk to. I don't know anyone around here."

"Doesn't your sister live close? If I remember correctly, she goes to Stanford?"

"Yeah, she did. She graduated last month. She actually just left to do something with the rain forests in South America. I'm not exactly sure what she's doing though. To be honest, the position sounds a little shady. It's something about working on local legislation to stop deforestation, but I can't figure out who she's actually working for though."

He nods. "You need to tell her to be extremely cautious. Many parts of South America are in a bit of distress right now with impeached presidents and corruption. Plus, they have that virus down there. Not to mention, if she's standing up to the big businesses that profit from the destruction of forests, she could be putting herself in danger."

Shrugging, I agree with him, "I know. But you don't know Georgia. She's a force of nature herself. She's adventurous and fearless. All the stuff you just mentioned probably makes her want to go work in that part of the world even more. She would never let risks or fear dictate her life. It's just who she is. She's brave." Some days, I wish I had a little bit of Georgia in me.

"Sounds like you two are a lot alike," Brad says.

I scoff. "We are nothing alike. I'm sure she's happy down there, living in some run-down shack. I would hate that. I'm way more materialistic than she is and a hell of a lot less brave."

"There's nothing wrong with liking the finer things in life, and I'd say you're very brave. You dropped everything and moved to a city where you didn't know anyone to chase your dream." His lips turn up in a grin.

I shake my head. "I didn't call you because I was being brave."

"Then, why did you call me, London?"

I sigh. "Because I was desperate."

"For those who are strong, a desperate situation is followed by a brave act. You are a strong woman, London. I can see it in you."

I don't know what to say to follow his comment, so instead, I bring my wine glass to my lips and let the rest of the crimson liquid slide down my throat in one long gulp.

Damn it.

As Brad moves to refill my glass, I hold my hand out to indicate that I don't need any more wine. "Really, I have to work tomorrow. I'm all set." The last thing I need to do is get wasted in front of my new boss.

"All right." The corners of his mouth tilt up, and he finishes filling my glass.

I'm not drinking it, I promise myself.

I lead the conversation toward safer topics and enjoy an incredible crème brûlée for dessert. We mix business and pleasure, laughing over some of Paige and my escapades and talking about some news stories slotted for this week. Overall, it's a great time, and I feel happy.

Before I know it, Brad is pulling up to the front of my hotel. The valet approaches Brad's car and opens the door to let me out.

"Thank you for dinner, boss. See you tomorrow." I grin.

"You're most welcome." He smiles back.

I stand and exit his car, shutting the door.

The passenger window rolls down. "Oh, London?" he calls from within.

"Yeah?" I bend down and peer into his vehicle.

His intense gaze grabs ahold of me and does all sorts of crazy things to my insides.

Damn you, Brad Pitt!

"I just thought you should know that, although I didn't ask you to, it doesn't mean that it won't be happening."

I tilt my head in question, and then my eyes widen with understanding.

Brad gives me a cocky grin, and before I can respond, he and his fancy sports car peel out onto the road.

I watch, my mouth agape, as his car fades into the distance, and I wonder what the hell I have gotten myself into.

TEN

Loïc

"For me, life is simply about survival."
—*Loïc Berkeley*

The loud boom comes out of nowhere. My heart leaps into my throat as I dive toward the nearest cover I can find, which happens to be a light pole. Leaning my back against the pole, I slide down until I'm sitting on the grass. My arms wrap around my head that's burrowed against my knees.

I cower, my body in a tight ball of fear. Adrenaline and a heavy dose of panic course through my veins as my brain tries to make sense of my surroundings. I take in breaths, pulling the air deep into my lungs, willing my body to stop shaking.

And I see it all again…

The grenade.

Cooper's face, full of determination and regret. But not regret for his actions. No, he would never be sorry for those. He would save his brothers again, if given the choice. No, in his face, I see sorrow for all those who, in that split-second decision, he was saying good-bye to. I see the grief as he accepted his fate and that of his loved ones.

The explosion.

My screams.

The pieces as he was blown apart.

I hit the wall, and the blackness comes.

But it doesn't stay.

It's followed by the pain, the sheer torturous ache that will never leave.

I want the blackness again. I want it to pull me under its depths and never let me surface.

Take me away.

Please take me away…

"Loïc?" a familiar voice questions hesitantly. "Loïc? Are you okay?"

Maggie?

Her voice is so out of place in this hell. She doesn't belong here.

"Loïc." This time, her voice is soft, soothing, but there's an urgent undertone present.

Opening my eyes, I take stock of my surroundings. It's dark. Releasing the position my body is in, I release a weary sigh. Slowly, I lift my head, pulling it away from my knees. When I blink, Maggie comes into focus.

"Loïc, are you okay?" Her words quiver now as unshed tears fill her eyes.

I'm scaring her.

"Yeah." I slowly nod my head. "Yeah, I'm fine."

I try to remember why I'm crouched under a pole on a patch of grass that separates the sidewalk and the street. Then, I recall the loud boom.

Damn fireworks.

Independence Day isn't for another week, yet the nightly cracks, pops, and explosions have already started. This isn't the first time I've lost myself to fear because of the noises. They take me back to my nightmare, and it feels like it's happening all over again.

I can manage it a little better now from home. This one caught me off guard. I can count on one hand the amount of times I've left my house since returning home two months ago. I didn't want to leave my house tonight, but Maggie wanted to meet up for a quick dinner after her shift. I couldn't say no because it's Maggie, but I should have.

Just look at me.

"Why are you on the ground?" Maggie asks, concerned.

"I'm…it's…" I release a long sigh, not knowing what to say. "I need to go home."

"Of course. Yes, let's go back to your place. No problem." Maggie extends her hand, and I take it. Once I'm standing, she says, "I'll drive. We'll get your truck later."

"Okay," I agree, knowing I'm in no shape to drive right now anyway.

Maggie grabs my arm, and the two of us walk toward the parking garage where she left her car. She doesn't say anything, but every minute or so, she gives my hand a gentle squeeze to reassure me that she's here. I'm grateful for the silence.

Once I'm back in my house, more of my anxiety leaves me.

"I know you're probably starving. We have some leftovers. Sarah made a huge chicken potpie last night. It's good. She's becoming a great cook," I offer as I take a seat at the kitchen table.

"Where is Sarah?" Maggie asks as she opens the fridge.

"At work. She's waitressing at that new barbeque restaurant downtown."

"How can she be on her feet all day like that when she's so pregnant?" Maggie pulls the glass container of food out of the refrigerator and places it on the counter.

"I don't know. I've asked her the same thing. She doesn't have to work right now. I have enough money for all of our bills. But she likes it."

"All right. Well, I guess she knows what her body can handle." Maggie places the food in the microwave. "Has she decided on a name yet?"

"Oh no…please don't…" I protest.

She laughs. "That bad?"

"Yes, that bad. It's all she ever talks about. It's driving me crazy. Do yourself a favor. Next time you see her, steer clear of the whole *name* topic."

"Okay." She chuckles. She places two plates of potpie on the table and sits down across from me. She takes a big bite. "This is good." She nods her head.

"Yeah," I agree.

After a few moments filled with only the sound of us eating, Maggie says, "So, how are you, Loïc?"

I'm sure she realizes that I'm not perfect, given the position she found me in, but I answer, "I'm okay."

"Is there anything I can do to help you?"

"No, I'm getting there. It's just an adjustment, is all." I shrug.

"Have you been seeing a therapist or anyone at the VA?"

"I don't need to talk to a head doctor, Maggie. I'm fine. It just takes a while to get back to normal; that's all."

Maggie places her fork down on the plate and looks me in the eyes. "I'm worried about you, Loïc."

"I know you are, but you don't need to be. I'm fine. I'm good." I offer her a smile.

"Well, please promise me that, if you're not, you'll go and get help."

"Of course."

"Loïc, promise me."

"I promise, okay?" I stare in her eyes, pleading with her to drop this subject.

She sighs. "All right. So, how is everything else?"

"Fine. Not much new. I hang out here all day, watch loads of TV. Sarah works a lot. When she's here, she's talking, usually about the baby. She feeds me way more than I need. And that's about it. That's my life. What about you? What have you been up to?"

Maggie releases the bottom lip that she's been biting. "My life isn't too exciting either. I'm either working or sleeping. I pick up extra shifts all the time, and when I'm at my parents' house, I'm asleep."

"What are you going to do with all your money?" I ask.

"Right now, it's just sitting in the bank. Maybe, when things get a little easier, I can use it to put a down payment on a house. I'm not sure yet."

"Yeah." I nod.

"So, have you spoken to London lately?" Maggie questions.

I shake my head. "Nope. Not since I called her and officially broke it off."

She drops her eyes to her plate.

"Look, I know I owe her more, Maggie. But I just can't right now. Don't be disappointed in me."

"I'm not, Loïc," she says reassuringly. "I know that everyone handles grief differently. You have to do what's best for you. I just really liked you two together."

I don't respond to her last statement. "Well, you two are still friends. Have you told her everything?"

"I haven't told her anything about you, Loïc. She doesn't know any of the details."

"Why not?"

"Because it's not my story to tell. What you went through is a huge deal, and it's very personal. It's your story to share."

"Huh," I let out a small sound of understanding.

"Plus, we don't really talk much anymore. I wouldn't say we're friends exactly." Maggie shrugs.

"You don't have to stop being friends with her because of me."

"I know, and you're not the only reason really. I mean, friends are in our lives for a reason. Not all of them are meant to be forever friends, right? I love London. She's a great person. But our friendship just doesn't work anymore. There are too many awkward silences, too many things we can't talk about, you know?"

"I can see that. So, when's the last time you spoke to her?"

"I haven't spoken to her much since you broke up with her. But she did call me last week to say good-bye."

"Good-bye?" I question.

"Yeah, she moved to Los Angeles. She got a new job out there. She sounded happy about it."

"Oh. Well, that's good."

This is the most I've been able to talk about London since I got back. I'd be lying if I said it didn't sting a little that she's gone, but I know it's probably for the best—for both of us.

I hope London is happy. She deserves it. I've come to the realization that happiness is no longer on my radar. For me, life is simply about survival. I need to find the courage to make it to tomorrow and the day after that and the day after that.

I feel like my life has been a constant battle ever since the day I lost my parents at the age of seven. Some days, I don't feel like fighting this battle anymore. I'm so tired. But it's on those days that I know I have to dig deeper and push through it with the hope that it won't always be this hard.

ELEVEN

London

*"Loïc's with me always, yet the weight of
his absence is paralyzing."*
—London Wright

"Three weeks!" I scream at my computer screen. "Three weeks!"

"I know. I'm sorry, Londy," my sister's cheerful tan face speaks to me on the screen. "I didn't mean to worry you or Mom and Dad."

"Then, you shouldn't have gallivanted off to a Third World country and left us hanging for three weeks with no word, George. That's twenty-one long-ass days we had to worry about you," I huff out.

"I understand, and I'm sorry. First of all, I don't think Brazil is a Third World country."

"Well, it's certainly not the Hills, Georgia."

"It's not like I'm in a war zone. You guys worry too much. This is the earliest I could get access to the Internet."

"I know they have Internet cafés down there—at least in the bigger cities," I argue.

"Yes, and the two that I came across were closed down."

"Well, that sounds promising," I scoff.

"Would you stop?" Georgia chuckles.

"What about your cell? Don't they have any towers down there?"

"I dropped it in the Amazon River and haven't gotten a new one yet," she says casually.

"You dropped your cell phone in the Amazon River?" I repeat, realizing how crazy that sounds.

"Yeah, I met this guy, Paco, down in the *mercado* the first day I was here. He said that he had a small boat and could take me out on the river, so of course, I said yes. Well, we saw this black caiman on the bank, which is like their equivalent of an alligator. I was leaning over the boat, taking its picture, and my foot slipped. I caught myself, but in the process, I dropped my phone."

I cover my face with my hands. "And, now, I have to worry about you getting eaten by alligators and piranhas. Just lovely."

"Stop. I've apologized. I'm safe. Now, let's move on to the important stuff." She grins. "How's your new job?"

"It's great."

"How's Brad Pitt?" She quirks up an eyebrow, causing me to laugh.

"Brad is fine. He's my boss. It's totally professional."

"Yeah, right. I saw him looking at you on New Year's. He wants to professionally bend you over his expensive desk and take you from behind."

I throw my head back in laughter. "Well, when we went out for dinner on my first full day here, he did say something about how we'd end up sleeping together."

"Ha! I knew it. Ooh…you can live out the hot-boss scenario. You know, doing it in his office and stuff."

I shake my head. "I'm not going to do that."

"Why not? You're single. He's hot. Live it up."

"First, because this job means a lot to me, and I don't want to mess it up. Second, because I don't want a relationship with him."

"Londy, I can guarantee he doesn't want a relationship either. A little bit of hot sex won't hurt." She winks, sporting a mischievous grin.

"No, I can't."

Just thinking about sex makes me feel guilty, like I'm being unfaithful to Loïc.

"You're single, babe. You have every right to do what you want with who you want." Georgia gives me a knowing stare through the computer screen.

"I know. I'm just not ready," I admit as the ever-present pang in my chest intensifies.

"All right." Georgia shoots me a kind smile before she squints toward the screen. "Where are you, by the way?"

I laugh, looking around the room with the bright green walls. "My new bedroom. It needs a paint job."

"Dad picked out this place?" she questions skeptically.

"No." I shake my head. "I told him that I didn't need him buying me an apartment. I'm renting this one with a girl from work. I want to start doing things on my own, you know?"

"Aw, my big sister is growing up!" Georgia says. "I can't believe you're sleeping in a room with that shade of green though. I've seen a couple of tree frogs that color down here."

"I might be growing up, but I still have taste. The second I have a free day, I'm going to paint it. I've just been working so much."

"You mean, you're going to hire a painter?" Georgia puckers her lips in question.

I roll my eyes. "Yes, I'll probably hire a painter. Rome wasn't built in a day." I stick out my tongue.

"Aw, if you were Paige, you would have said, *Detroit was built in a day*, or, *The grass is greener on the other side*, or something equally ridiculous."

We both smile.

"How is Paige?" she asks.

"She's good. Just working a lot. She loves her job."

"Oh, that's great. Do you miss her?"

"Honestly, I really haven't had much of a chance to. I'm so busy here. Plus, Kate is, like, the friendliest person in the world. She never lets me feel lonely."

"Who's Kate?"

"Oh, my new roommate. She's the receptionist at work. She's from Biloxi, Mississippi, and she is the nicest person. I really like her."

"Oh, awesome."

"So, how is work going for you?" I ask.

"It's okay. It's frustrating because I feel like I'm not making much headway, but I'm trying."

"Listen, George, I was watching a documentary the other day—"

"Wait. You were watching a documentary? Who are you?" Georgia laughs.

I chuckle. "Well, actually, Kate was watching it. I was in my room, watching *Friends* on Netflix, but when I came out to get a drink, I had to stay and watch it with her. It was so interesting. So, anyway, the whole documentary was about the meat industry and how it's destroying the environment. Well, they talked a lot about the rain forests and said that people who have stood up for the rain forests against these big cattle companies have been found dead. That's some scary stuff, Georgia. I don't really think you should be doing that. Come home. It's too dangerous. It's not worth your life."

"I'll be fine," Georgia says, giving me a feeble attempt of reassurance.

"You don't know that. Just come home," I plead.

"London, people die every day from bee stings. Does that mean I should never risk going outside again, in fear of being stung? People also die in car crashes every day. Should I never get in a vehicle again? People die from food poisoning. Should I not eat?"

"That's different," I argue.

"Not really. There are a million ways in which I could die. I can't live my life in fear of death, London. That's no way to live."

"But you're putting yourself in danger."

"Maybe a tad," she says. "But it's for something that matters. If I die from trying to protect something that I believe in, then it will not be for nothing. You know? London, I only get one life. I'm going to live it to the fullest and without fear. And maybe, just maybe, I'll leave the world a little better off because of my efforts."

"Georgia," I beg.

"Listen, I'm a smart girl. I'm not going to put myself in a situation where I think there is a direct threat. I feel very safe down here. I'm not worried. Please don't spend your time worrying about me. Okay?"

"Pfft, tell that to Mom. She's so busy trying to stay busy that she had an acroyoga tent built in her backyard.

She's gone yoga crazy, holding acro retreats and trainings at their house."

"Really? What does Dad say?"

"Oh, you know Dad. He doesn't have much to say about anything that makes Mom happy."

"That's hilarious," Georgia says.

"Well, if you're going to stay down there, you have to keep in regular contact, so we don't go crazy with worry."

"I can do that."

"That means, replace your phone."

"Got it." She nods. "Well, I should probably Skype Mom before she completely loses it."

"That might be a good idea," I agree with a grin. "I love you, George. Be safe."

"I love you, Londy. Make sure to remember to tell me all the details when Brad Pitt leans you over his desk and drives you home."

"You're ridiculous." I shake my head.

"I know." She lets out a short laugh.

"Bye."

"Bye."

I close my laptop screen with a smile. *I just love my sister.*

And, now, I miss Loïc...

Everything makes me miss him—when I feel love, when I'm sad, when I'm tired, or when the sky's blue. So, basically, always. The only time I don't hurt with longing is when I'm really occupied at work. Tasks that keep my mind busy are my best resources against fighting a broken heart.

I'm working my tail off with the paper, whipping out stories like nobody's business—partly to show Brad and everyone else that I'm a valuable member of the team and partly to keep busy.

I thought that moving to California would help me get over Loïc, and maybe it is. I just wish the process would happen a little faster.

Yes, I don't have to see the physical reminders of our relationship, like the restaurants we ate at, the park we ran around, or my old room where we spent a lot of time snuggled up together. Yet I've realized that I don't need those visuals to think of him because he's already a part of me.

He's everywhere—in my heart, my mind, and my dreams.

Loïc's with me always, yet the weight of his absence is paralyzing.

I left all the tokens from our relationship in my old room in Michigan—gifts he'd gotten me or little mementos of our time together—thinking it would be easier here without them. But, sometimes, I wish that I had something physical to hold, something real to mourn.

When I'm really desperate, like now, I close my eyes and picture his face. I can see it all so clearly—his ocean-blue eyes, tan skin, and the way his face lit up when he smiled at me. I press my fingers against my lips, trying to remember what his kiss felt like. I can barely remember. So, perhaps I am losing him. That thought doesn't bring me comfort, as it should. It just makes me sad.

A delicious aroma and a desire to escape my self-pity lure me from my bedroom. I find Kate cooking in the kitchen.

"What are you making?"

"Vegan enchiladas," Kate says.

She's been on a vegan kick ever since watching that documentary that I was telling Georgia about.

"They smell heavenly. What are the ingredients?"

"Corn tortillas, sweet potatoes, beans, onions, coconut milk, and spices," she answers.

"I can't wait to try them."

"I know. Me, too. When I was looking up recipes online, this recipe had almost all five stars, so it should be good."

"Awesome. What do you want to watch tonight?"

"You know, there's this new documentary out about the effects of GMOs," she says as she pulls a casserole dish out of the oven.

"Actually, I'm kind of in the mood for something lighter," I admit.

"That's fine. What were you thinking?"

"How about an episode or two of *Friends*?" I suggest.

"What's that?" Kate asks.

"You've seriously never heard of *Friends*?" I shoot her a look with wide eyes of shock.

"Um, no. Should I have?"

"Yes! It's only the best show of all time," I squeal. "It's a sitcom from the nineties."

Kate laughs. "Well, growing up, I wasn't allowed to watch TV. I watched my first TV show with my college roommate. It was *Grey's Anatomy*. I was pretty traumatized after it though." She chuckles. "I usually watch documentaries or movies, not a lot of TV."

"Oh my gosh…this is, like…" I think for a moment. "Amazing! We have to do an entire marathon, all ten seasons. You must experience it from the beginning," I say, trying not to shout at Kate with excitement.

"It's that good?" she asks with a smile as she starts to plate our dinner.

"It's the best show ever, Kate. Seriously. We were meant to be roommates. I can't believe you've lived your life without knowing *Friends*. This is going to be so much fun." I clap my hands together. "I'm going to go set up the series premiere."

I can't wait to tell Paige this. Not only is she *not* going to believe it, but she's also going to be jealous that I get to see it through the eyes of someone who's watching it for the first time.

For the first time in a long time, I feel genuinely happy. I know this initial giddiness is covering up my deep longing for Loïc—it never goes away, not even for a second—but I'll take it.

For the next several weeks, I'm going to be so busy with work and then a *Friends* marathon that my heart isn't going to have time to ache. I might be able to stretch the show out for over a month. Ten seasons is a lot when only watching it after work.

This is the best.

I know it's silly, and it's just a Band-Aid for my problems. Yet let's be real. How many times does a parent put a Band-Aid on a child because they physically need it? Sometimes, yes. But, much of the time, especially with the younger kids, it's mental. A Band-Aid makes a boo-boo feel better. *Friends* is my bandage. When the show's over, I know I'll have to rip it off, only to discover that all the hurt and pain are still right where I left them.

But, for now, I'm happy. And, as Rachel walks into that coffee shop in her rain-soaked wedding dress, I'm going to laugh alongside Kate and pretend that I'm healed.

TWELVE

Loïc

> *"I'm being dragged down by demons that
> I can't even pretend to know how to fight."*
> —Loïc Berkeley

"Why did Mommy and Daddy choose your name?"

*"You named me Loïc because it means warrior, and warriors
are strong," I repeat what they've told me many times.*

*"Not only are they strong, but they're also very brave, the
bravest. No matter what happens in your life, Loïc, you'll be strong
enough and brave enough to conquer it all. You were already more
courageous than Daddy when you were one day old. Strength isn't
measured by how many muscles you have or what you are or are not
afraid of. Strength comes from within. It comes from your heart. It
will give you courage to face things, even when you're afraid."*

"I'm so afraid," I answer honestly.

*I reach my hand out, and Daddy takes it in his. His is so
much bigger than mine.*

"Be brave, Loïc."

"I can't." I feel my lip tremble and try hard not to cry.

"You already are." Daddy leans down and gives me a kiss. "You, my little warrior, have the biggest heart I know, and that makes you the bravest."

Then, Daddy's gone. It's all black and so scary.

"Daddy!" I cry into the darkness.

"Loïc, dear, why the tears?" Nan walks into my room, bringing light with her.

"Nan, Daddy left!" I scream out.

"Oh, love. No, he didn't. Where did I tell you that magic lives?"

"In here." I touch a finger to my head. "And in here." I place my hand over my heart.

She nods, her gentle smile on her face. "That's right." Her eyes go wide with happiness, like they always do when she's telling me something exciting. "Guess where the ones we love live forever?"

She expectantly looks at me as I think about her question.

"In here." I touch a finger to my head. "And in here." I place my hand over my heart.

"That's right." She nods her head, pleased. "The ones you love never leave you. You can always find them in your mind and heart. Just be still and listen. Now, I'm going to tell you something I told your daddy when he was your age, and I want you to really listen, okay?"

I nod my head.

"Life is one big adventure. You only get one life, so you have to make it count. You can't sit around on your bum, waiting for joy to find you. We're all born with the capacity to live incredible lives, but the trick is…you have to work for it. A magical life is within everyone's grasp, but you have to make it happen for yourself. Everything that is worth having requires effort. Happiness will always be there for you, but it's not free. Do you understand?"

I'm quiet for a moment before saying, "I think so."

"You will, Loïc, love. Just remember...make your life count, and please be happy. Promise me," she urges, her blue eyes filling with tears.

"I promise, Nan. I promise."

"That's my boy."

I bolt up with a start, forcing my eyes to blink, and the room comes into focus. The dim light of the alarm clock saturates the space with a soft glow, allowing me to figure out where I am.

In my room.

The voices of my grandma and my dad still echo through my mind, clearer than they have been in years.

Jesus.

I run my fingers through my damp hair.

"Hello?" I whisper into the night. A foreboding sense that I'm not alone weighs heavily on me. "Sarah?" I say softly.

But there's no response.

No one's here.

My stare finds my door closed, exactly as it should be.

Be brave.

Be happy.

Be strong.

The voices are so loud. They pound through my mind, demanding to be heard. Pressing the palms of my hands against my ears, I try to block them out.

I feel so...

Wait.

I feel.

Moving my hands down to my chest, I press them against my heart, the epicenter of the current anguish that's moving through my body like a raging fire, an inferno of pain.

The ache doesn't solely consist of hurt. There's love, remorse, sorrow, and longing. But what resonates with me the most is the fact that I can feel it all. The gravity of these emotions has overpowered the vast numbness that I've been living under for so long.

And then it happens.

My chest heaves, my muscles constrict, and my shoulders shake as I cry.

After all this time, I motherfucking cry.

The warm tears course down my face in streams. I can taste the saltiness as they cascade over my mouth.

I welcome it all, despite the acute pain it brings. I need it to remember what it's like to feel again.

The only thing worse than experiencing this amount of anguish is not feeling anything at all. The black hole of emptiness is worse than all the emotions put together. I've been so empty, a mere shell of myself, barely a man. I was fading into oblivion, and I didn't care, not one bit.

Every thought, face, and memory tears through my brain, spreading hope and a burning ache in my chest. But maybe that's the way it goes. I have to hold on to my greatest memories to give me strength to live again even though they all—every last one—bring an enormous amount of agony.

I think of my parents and grandparents and how very much I loved them and how much they loved me. Even now, almost twenty years later, their love is saving me when I need it the most.

I think of Cooper, my best friend, my brother. He loved me when I was unlovable. He saw something in me that I couldn't see in myself. He didn't give up until I let him in. He was my family since the moment we'd become friends. He protected me more times in my adult life than I can count—or even recognize, for that matter. Let's face it; without Cooper, who knows where I'd be? He came into my life when I needed the support of another person more than anything. He was saving me up until the very end.

He saved me.

Finally, I think of London, the enigma that she is—as feisty as she is beautiful. She wiggled her way into my heart with the tenacity of a lion, and she loved me fiercely. The time I spent with London was the happiest I've ever been in my entire life.

I feel a lot of things, but what I feel that I never thought I'd feel again is hope.

My sobs continue as months—no, make that *years* of pain escape. I cry for all those I have lost, and most importantly, I finally cry for myself. I realize that the only way to heal is to acknowledge the grief. I will never be able to move on if I don't allow my pain to surface. I need to feel it, accept it, own it, and then I need to let it go.

Can I?

Am I brave enough?

Hell yes. I'm a fighter.

I always have been, and I always will be. But I know I can't do it on my own.

Sarah rushes into my room, her hair a tangled mess and her face tired from sleep. "Loïc!" she shrieks, worry etched into her features. "What's wrong? Are you okay?"

She rushes to my bed and sits beside me. Wrapping her arms around me, she holds me tight. I rest my face against her shoulder as a few errant tears continue to fall.

"Shh…" She runs her fingers through my hair. "It's okay. Everything will be fine. Whatever it is, we can figure it out. I love you, Loïc. You're going to be okay." She continues to repeat soothing words as she absentmindedly rocks me against her, like a mother would her child.

I hold her tight, allowing her presence to calm me. I'm suddenly hit by an immense feeling of gratitude for Lieutenant Dixon for insisting that I allow one person in because, right now, I'm so grateful to have her.

"I need help, Sarah," I choke out.

"Okay, tell me what to do," she says reassuringly.

"I need professional help. I can't do it on my own. There's too much darkness," I admit out loud.

It's now that I realize that the helplessness, gloom, and despair that have been plaguing my daily thoughts are more than grief. I'm being dragged down by demons that I can't even pretend to know how to fight.

"Absolutely. Let's get dressed and go to the VA. We'll get you help. It's going to be okay. I love you, Loïc." She kisses me on the forehead and stands.

"But it's early," I say.

"It's fine. We'll stop and eat a good breakfast beforehand. Plus, the ER area is open twenty-four hours a day." She gives me a warm smile.

"How do you know they have an ER area?"

"I've done some research. I've actually been there to make sure I knew where all the departments were and what the procedures would be for when you wanted to go," she says with a shrug of her shoulders.

"Really?" I ask in disbelief.

"Of course. I'm your person, Loïc. I'm going to do everything I can to make sure you're okay. I knew you'd be ready to go in on your own time."

"Oh." I swing my leg over the side of the bed. "Should we call to make an appointment or something?" I reach for my prosthetic.

"Nope. We just show up. They have a policy that they won't turn away any veteran. You will be seen today. They will talk to you, look at your records, and develop your treatment plan, including medications and therapy sessions. If you feel like you're a danger to yourself or others, they'll admit you."

"I'm not going to hurt anyone, including myself."

"I know, but it's not uncommon, Loïc. If you felt like you might, it would be okay. No one would judge you."

"I'm not suicidal," I state clearly as I pull the plastic sleeve of my prosthetic leg over my stump.

"Okay." She smiles, placing her hand on my shoulder and supplying a gentle squeeze. "I'm going to throw my hair up and get dressed. Then, I'll be out in the living room when you're ready to go."

I nod once, and she exits my room.

I don't know exactly what to expect out of today, but this is the most hopeful I've felt in a while.

Everything that my therapists told me when I was recovering both in Germany and Washington, DC, is coming back now. For whatever reason, possibly my own stubborn nature or perhaps due to the amount of darkness that had already grabbed hold of me, I couldn't hear their words then. I couldn't listen.

Now, I'm ready. I've found the strength to fight for myself. I'm a damaged man, no doubt. Maybe I'll never be the person I was before this last tour in Afghanistan, but I have to try.

I have to put in the work to heal my mind so that I can function. Not a day goes by when I don't wish that

Cooper were here and not me. But that's simply not the reality of it. He's gone, and for some reason, I'm not.

And, though it will be difficult, I need to learn how to show up and be present.

It's time I fight to live.

THIRTEEN

London

> *"It's not the kiss I crave*
> *but the soul connected to it."*
> —*London Wright*

A miscalculated flick of my paintbrush against the wall sends a firestorm of gray droplets toward my face. "Kate!" I whine to my roommate.

She takes one look at my speckled face and bursts into laughter.

"It's not funny. This'd better come out of my hair," I grumble.

"Oh, bless your heart." She shakes her head from side to side, a giant smile on her face.

"Um, isn't that the equivalent of saying, *Fuck you*, or something in the South?" I ask, quirking up an eyebrow in question.

"It can be. Just depends on the manner in which it's said. I didn't mean it that way, of course. I meant it literally because you, London, are just the cutest. I've never met someone quite like you." She chuckles to herself and continues painting.

"I really think that we should've paid someone to do this. I've never painted a thing in my life." I set my brush in the bucket and walk over to the kitchen to grab a paper towel.

"Exactly. You came to LA for a new life, for new experiences. It's time you step out of your comfort zone and try new things," Kate says.

After quickly running the paper towel under the water, I drag the damp paper across my paint-splattered face. "But I am getting lots of new experiences in. I don't think that painting an entire apartment needs to be one of them."

"You said that you wanted to be independent. Independent people paint their own walls, London."

"I don't necessarily agree with that. Why are there so many painters then?" I don't wait for Kate to respond, so I continue, "Because tons of people hire them to paint; that's why. I wasn't going to use my trust fund. I was going to use the money I've made on my own. That's being grown-up. There is nothing wrong with hiring someone to help with things that I know I'm not good at. Plus, it's good for the economy. How are painters supposed to feed their families if everyone does their own painting?" I send Kate a pointed look.

"You can argue your case; I'll give ya that. But you told me to help you be independent, and that is what I'm doing. You should have to paint your own place at least once. Consider it a rite of passage. Plus, we're on the last room. At this point, you just need to suck it up, buttercup."

"Huh," I huff as I grab my paintbrush from the can of paint. I continue painting over the bright yellow walls of the living room. "Who lived here before you anyway? A circus clown?"

"I don't know, but whoever it was sure had interesting taste." Kate giggles.

"Part of me thought it would be funny to leave it the way it was for Paige to see. But I think I'm more excited for her to see the finished look."

Paige is coming to visit next weekend, and Kate and I have been getting our apartment ready for company, decorating it to our tastes. Kate took me on an adventure known as thrift-store shopping. I've never purchased anything from a secondhand store, but last weekend's shopping extravaganza was so much fun. It's amazing what one can find at those places. We found treasures, like a ceramic elephant playing the clarinet and a coatrack shaped like a naked woman—both of which, we did not buy. We did buy a gorgeous aqua blown-glass vase and an antique apothecary table though.

We decided to go with an ocean chic décor. After we finish this last room, our apartment will be painted in all earthy cream and gray hues with blue and teal accent items throughout.

It's looking awesome. I have to admit, as much as I complain, it's pretty gratifying to complete a project from start to finish and have it turn out so great. The cherry on top is that it's kept my mind busy, which is always a good thing.

I've been in LA now for a little over two months. August in Cali has been pretty much like August in Michigan—hot. Next weekend is Labor Day weekend, and I can't wait to spend three days with Paige. It would be even better if Georgia could be here with us, but besides a proof-of-life text every few days, I haven't gotten to speak with her much this summer. She's busy with saving the world, one tree at a time.

"So, what's the deal with you and Brad anyway?" Kate asks, pulling me from my thoughts.

"What do you mean?"

"Come on. The entire floor has been talking about it. Everyone thinks something is going on between you two. As your roommate, I've been waiting for you to spill the beans, but since you haven't, I figured I'd just ask you."

After finishing the edging on my portion of the wall, I grab the paint roller to finish the rest. "Nothing is going on between us."

"London…" Kate lowers her voice, like my mother always does when she's trying to get us to come clean with a lie.

"Kate…" I imitate her.

"If you want it to be a secret, I won't tell anyone. You know you can trust me."

"I'm serious, Kate. Nothing is going on between Brad and me. We have a boss-employee relationship and nothing more. I promise."

"So, you don't have any interest in him?" She doesn't sound convinced.

"No, not at all."

"Well, I don't think it's the same for him. You do realize that you're the only writer he has daily meetings with?"

"That can't be true." I stop rolling to think about whether or not I've noticed him meeting with others. But, honestly, I don't really keep tabs on his daily activities.

"It is true. He meets with everyone at our morning meetings, which is where everything is discussed and finalized. If the other writers have a question, they'll go to him, of course, but he definitely doesn't meet with them separately and every day, like he does with you."

"Really? Wow, I had no idea that he meets with me more. I mean, I know he's attracted to me—I'm not naive—but I didn't realize that he treated me differently than the other writers." I bring the back of my hand to my forehead. "Ugh, I feel stupid. Everyone at work probably thinks I'm a tramp."

Kate laughs. "No, they don't."

"Yeah, right. I guarantee they think Brad and I are humping like bunnies during our 'daily meetings.'" I use my fingers to make quotations in the air.

"Who cares what others think?"

"I do, Kate. I don't want everyone thinking that I slept my way into this job. I work really hard and write damn good articles. I want to be taken seriously. Maybe you should tell them that I'm not sleeping with Brad," I suggest, trying to figure out how to do serious damage control.

"I can when it comes up. But people are going to believe what they want. I wouldn't worry too much about it, London. Actions speak louder than words. Just keep doing your best work and show everyone what you're made of. Even if they think you and Brad are together, they're not going to be able to deny your talent." Kate takes a second to admire the wall she just painted before coming over to help me finish mine.

"I'm going to tell Brad to stop treating me differently than other employees. That guy…" I shake my head with a scowl.

"That'd probably be a good idea. I mean, if you wanted to be with him, that's totally your call. But, if you don't, you should set some parameters."

"I thought I had." I roll my eyes. "I told him from the start that I wouldn't sleep with him."

I'll definitely have a few choice words for Brad when I see him tomorrow. *Ugh, making all my coworkers think we're sleeping together. What an ass.*

I drop the paint roller in the pail with a thud. I hope I never have to touch one of those again in my lifetime. My back aches, and my shoulders are screaming in pain. To think of it, my entire body is sore and fatigued. I'm not a manual-labor kind of girl, and I'm okay with that.

I plop down onto our new cream-colored sectional although it's currently covered in drop cloths to protect it from paint splatter. Leaning my head back, I admire our walls. "We did a really good job," I say.

"We sure did," Kate agrees from beside me. "You want to clean up really quick and set everything up?"

"Sure."

Kate is the first to venture off the couch. She extends her hand, and I take it. "Then, we'll order takeout and veg for the rest of the day." She helps me up.

"Do you want to start *How I Met Your Mother* today?" I ask her.

We finished our *Friends* marathon a couple of weeks ago. I told her we should start *How I Met Your Mother* next. Although it's not *Friends*, it's a really close second.

"Yeah, that sounds good," Kate agrees.

I enter Brad's office for our daily meeting.

"Please shut the door." He motions toward the open doorway.

I comply with his request before sitting down in one of the chairs in front of his desk. "Good morning," I say to him, my tone overly sweet.

He closes the laptop in front of himself and gives me his full attention. "Did you have a good weekend?" he asks with his dreamy smile.

"Very good. Thank you," I say shortly.

Our conversations are usually much more friendly, but this morning, I'm pissed.

"Is everything all right, London?"

"Not really, Brad. You see, apparently, the entire staff here thinks that our daily private meetings are booty calls." I hold back a smile when his eyes widen. I continue in my business tone, "It has come to my attention that I'm the only one on your staff who you meet with daily, and I'd like to inquire as to why that is."

Brad presses a finger to his lips where a small smile is present. He assesses me before answering, "Well, you're one of the newer writers, and I wanted to make sure you were getting all your questions answered to ensure your success with the paper. We don't have an official mentoring program, so I've seen our meetings as such."

"As mentoring opportunities?" I question with a quirk of my eyebrow.

He nods. "Yes."

"Interesting. Well, I spoke with Scott, the writer in *Sports* who started two weeks ago, and he tells me that you haven't requested one meeting with him. Does he not deserve these mentor meetings?"

"London, what is this really about?" Brad asks with a sigh.

"I want to know why you have been treating me differently? Apparently, the office thinks I'm easy, and you're to blame." I glare toward him.

"No one thinks that," he says with a shake of his head and a slight smile.

"They might as well. They think we're doing it." I cross my arms in front of my chest.

Brad leans forward, resting his arms on his desk. "So what if they do? Who cares?"

"Oh my goodness…I care, Brad." I try to contain the high-pitched squeal of my voice.

"All right, fine." He pauses. "I hold meetings with you every day because I like seeing you."

"Okay?" I question, the word coming out slowly.

Brad stands and walks around his desk. He reaches out his hand toward me, palm up, in an open invitation. I hesitantly take it and allow him to pull me up from the chair. He stands mere inches in front of me, still holding my hand.

Having him so close in proximity, I can't help but take in his scent. I can't put my finger on the type of cologne he's wearing, but I can guarantee that it doesn't smell half as intoxicating on anyone else as it does on him.

I can feel my heart beating rapidly within my chest. My stomach flips, like butterflies are competing in their own version of gymnastics. I loathe the way my body reacts to him. It's strictly visceral, not something I plan or even want. Yet the attraction's there, and he knows it.

"London…" he whispers in my ear, leaning down and still holding my hand.

My eyes clamp shut with his closeness, and goose bumps explode over my skin, causing a quick shiver to shoot through my body.

"I like you. And I know you like me. Let's stop playing games."

"I'm not playing games." My voice comes out soft and shaky.

"London, open your eyes, and look at me," his deep timbre instructs.

I shake my head.

That's when I feel his soft, full lips cover mine.

All summer, I've been trying to remember what it was like to kiss Loïc, to feel his lips on mine. I've all but forgotten the way his lips felt. The last time they touched mine was nine long months ago when they kissed me good-bye right before he left on the trip that would change everything.

The last time Loïc's lips touched mine was so much more than a kiss. It was a promise of love and commitment. It was a promise to return to me. But, though he came back, he never came back to me.

And, now, my lips that have longed to be kissed every minute of every day for the last nine months are being kissed, and it hurts.

It feels wrong and painful.

It's not the kiss I crave but the soul connected to it. I miss the love and connection I feel for one man only, and it's not this one.

"Stop." I pull away, a guilty tear rolling down my cheek. "I love someone else, Brad. You can't do that again."

"I thought you were single." He lets go of my hand.

"I am, but..." I stop, not wanting to say any more.

"You're in love with a man who doesn't want you?"

I don't respond.

"I'm being rejected because you have feelings for someone who doesn't love you back? Seriously, London?" His voice carries an edge of anger.

"I came here for a job, Brad, not a relationship or a fuck buddy or wherever else you see this going. I just want to write. I don't want you treating me differently than everyone else. And I don't want your lips or any other part of your body to touch me again. Are we clear?"

I turn and all but stomp toward the door.

Before I open it, I address Brad one more time, "You might have offered me this job because you wanted to get in my pants. But I hope you've been reading my articles because they're good. And, unless you need to talk to me about something legitimate, I expect all future work-related topics to be covered in our morning staff meetings."

I give him a big smile—albeit a forced one—and I exit his office.

FOURTEEN

Loïc

> *"The people we love most in this world*
> *are the ones who have the capacity*
> *to cause us the most pain."*
> —*Loïc Berkeley*

"He hates me! He hasn't even met me, and he hates me already!" a very pregnant Sarah cries as she lies, sprawled out, on the couch, fanning herself with the gossip magazine that came in the mail today.

"Do you want me to turn down the air some more?" I ask her even though it already feels like the Arctic tundra in here.

"Why does he hate me, Loïc?" she continues her rant.

"How about a fan?" I suggest.

I leave Sarah to wallow in her uncomfortable pregnancy alone for a moment and make my way toward the stairs to the basement.

Closing my eyes, I pull in a few deep breaths before turning the handle. I haven't stepped a foot in the basement since I've been home.

We never used the basement for hanging out. Instead, it has always been one giant storage area for anything and everything. I don't know how much of Cooper's random stuff Maggie took, but I'm guessing, not all of it. The fear of not knowing what I could find down these steps has stopped me from going down them before. But it's time.

We had several fans, none of which I've seen since I returned, so I'm thinking that Maggie put them down here to store over the winter when Cooper and I were deployed.

It's just stuff, I tell myself as I descend the stairs.

Two months ago, I wouldn't have attempted this, knowing that being confronted with something of Cooper's could have sent me into a full-blown panic attack. But, ever since that night a month and a half ago, where I dreamed of my dad and Nan and then went to the VA with Sarah, life has been more manageable.

I'm currently going to therapy three times a week. I'm also on different medication that's been helping with my depression and PTSD. Yet I think what is helping the most are the weekly support groups that I've been going to with other wounded soldiers from Afghanistan and Iraq. They seem to understand what I'm going through more than the doctors ever could.

The past month has been, for all intents and purposes, pretty okay.

I hear a scream coming from Sarah. I immediately spot a fan and quickly grab it before heading back up the stairs.

Although my quality of life has been improving, Sarah's has been getting worse with each passing day of her pregnancy. She's currently ten days late and not very happy about it. She's definitely no longer in the glowing and happy stage of pregnancy. It's more like, *If this baby doesn't come out soon, I'm going to murder someone.*

"Are you okay?" I ask when I'm back upstairs.

I plug the fan in and set it on the end table, so it's blowing toward Sarah.

"Yeah, I'm fine. Just a stupid cramp. The fan feels good. Thanks," she says weakly.

"You're welcome."

"I'm so uncomfortable, Loïc. I can't find a position to lie in that will allow me to sleep. My whole body hurts, and I just want him out. Why isn't he coming out? I've tried to make him comfortable and happy in there. I love him. Why is he torturing me?" Sarah's voice is full of despair.

"You just have to make it to tomorrow. You'll see your doctor in the morning, and I'm sure she'll induce you," I offer.

"You think so?" Her voice is laced with hope.

"Yeah. Remember, at your appointment last week, she said she doesn't like to let babies go too much over ten days late? Well, tomorrow will be day eleven, so I bet she'll induce."

"She'd better. I'll have some choice words for her if she doesn't," Sarah says with a huff.

"I'm sure you will." I grin. "Can I get you anything? Are you thirsty?"

"I could go for some lemonade."

"On it."

"Thanks, Loïc."

"You're welcome," I say as I make my way to the kitchen.

I almost drop the pitcher of lemonade when Sarah screams again. Setting it down on the counter, I walk hastily toward the living room.

"What's wrong?"

"Oh, just another stupid cramp. I think, if I lie a certain way, I get them. They kill, but they don't last too long." She holds her belly.

"Sarah, I'm pretty sure those are contractions."

Her face shoots up to look at mine. "You think?"

"You're getting these cramps every few minutes, right?" I ask.

She nods. "Yeah."

"They're contractions. Let's grab your bag and get going. You're having this baby." I smile down to Sarah whose face shows utter shock and panic. "You're going to do great," I add.

"He hates me!" Sarah screams at the top of her lungs after a hard-fought push. She's drenched in sweat. Her body shakes with agony.

Using a cool cloth, I wipe her face that's dripping with a mixture of sweat and tears. "You're doing great, Sarah," I try to reassure her.

"I hate this," she cries. "It hurts so much. How can women do this every day?"

By the time we got to the hospital, Sarah was almost completely dilated. We weren't in the hospital room for more than thirty minutes before she started pushing. So, apparently, she had been having cramps for a while. The downside was that she was past the point to get an epidural, so she is having her first baby completely naturally, and she is quite upset about it.

"It will be over soon," I say soothingly.

"This baby hates me, Loïc. Why is he doing this to me?" Tears course down her face.

"Stop saying that. He does not." I hold back a grin. "This is just part of the process. I know he can't wait to get out of there to meet his mommy."

"Oh no." Sarah's face goes white in fear as another contraction starts.

"Time to push for a count of ten. Push," the doctor tells Sarah.

Sarah bears down, whimpering in pain, as the doctor counts back from ten to one. When the doctor reaches one, Sarah relaxes. Her now red face starts to lighten, and she cries. I hate seeing her in so much pain. I'm pretty sure that I'm praying for this to be over almost as hard as she is. Watching someone you love suffer is the definition of torture.

Sarah ends up pushing for an agonizing two hours before the baby finally slides out.

For as long as I live, I will never forget the sight of the doctor putting the wet little guy on Sarah's chest. The look on her face resonates with unconditional love. She sobs uncontrollably as she holds him to herself. And, this time, she is crying because the overwhelming love she feels needs to get out. She cries tears of love, relief, and joy.

She keeps repeating the words, "I love you. I love you. I love you," in between gently kissing him on his head.

She looks up at me. "He's perfect," she chokes out.

"He is," I agree. My eyes fill with unshed tears from the sight below me. "Just perfect, Sarah."

The nurse takes the baby to clean him up while the doctor tends to Sarah. I hold her hand, rubbing my thumb across her warm skin.

"You were amazing," I tell her, still in awe of what a woman goes through to bring a baby into the world.

"It hurt so bad. I think he's going to be an only child," she says, exhausted.

I laugh. "You say that now. You might change your mind."

There are a few moments where no words are spoken between us.

I think about love and loss. I think about Sarah as a mom. She will never be the same person she was yesterday. The type of love one feels for their child changes them. She'll spend the rest of her life walking around as if her heart were on the outside of her chest—fragile and exposed—always worrying for her child. I think that's how all parents feel—at least the good ones. And Sarah's going to be a great one.

I lightly squeeze Sarah's hand, and she opens her exhausted eyes.

"I think the people we love most in this world are the ones who have the capacity to cause us the most pain. This little boy is going to be the best thing to ever happen to you. I think you'll find you'd go through it all again, multiple times, to have him because on the other side of anguish is a powerful love."

"I think you're right." She smiles.

The nurse brings the baby over and places him in Sarah's arms. "He's just perfect," she says. "Eight pounds, two ounces and twenty inches long. He passed his exam with flying colors."

Tears fill Sarah's eyes once more, and I know how relieved she must feel.

"Do you want to hold him?" she asks me.

"Sure." I carefully take the baby from Sarah's arms and hold him in mine.

His eyes are open, but I can't make out the color. Right now, they're dark—a combination of blue, gray, and black. He's completely bald with faint wisps of white hair covering his scalp. I get the feeling he's going to be blond, like his mother.

I draw in a breath as an enormous wave of love envelops me. The precious boy grabs ahold of my pinkie with more force than such a tiny human should have. He's strong. He's perfect. And, though I've just met him, I know I'll love him forever.

"Do you want to hear his name?" Sarah asks.

"You decided?" I grin.

"I sure did. His name is Evan Loïc Berkeley."

"Evan," I say softly as baby Evan wraps his tiny fingers around my thumb.

"I couldn't get the name Evan out of my head. I kept coming back to it. And then, of course, I decided to name him after the man who has loved me more than anyone else. If you hadn't saved me over and over, I wouldn't even be here to be his mommy. I want him to be strong and brave, like you."

"Thank you, Sarah." I look to her beautiful but tired face.

It's hard to wrap my mind around everything she and I have gone through together. We've been through hell and back. Yet it was all worth it because, now, we have this little guy here.

"I'm going to be the best uncle ever," I say to her as I place Evan back in her arms.

"Yeah," she agrees softly.

But I don't miss the edge of disappointment I hear in her voice.

FIFTEEN

London

*"I don't want to be with anyone else
until I can give him my whole heart, and
right now, it belongs to someone else."*
—London Wright

The waiter refills my iced tea, and I thank him before I continue my conversation with Brad. I'm reading off the notes from my phone. "So, then I'll interview the parents and discuss her plans for Tokyo?"

"Yes, that sounds good," Brad answers.

I'm interviewing a swimmer from Los Angeles who won a gold medal at the summer Olympics in Rio. The title of the article is going to be "Life After the Games." Of course, I want to talk to her parents and get some sweet story from when she was young. Readers eat that stuff up. Maybe, if I'm lucky, I will score a photo of her at three with a swim cap on, and her parents will tell me, *Her very first words were gold medal.* I laugh to myself.

"What's so funny over there?" Brad asks from beside me.

"Nothing. Just thinking."

"You're going to have the shoe story ready, right?" he asks.

"Oh, yes. This story is right up my alley. You sure I shouldn't be buying a few pairs on the company's dime? You know, for research purposes." I give Brad a smirk.

It's the end of November, and shoppers have already started buying Christmas presents. I'm running a story on the most in-demand shoes and where to find them. Tomorrow, I'll get to spend my day going from boutique to boutique, checking out heels.

How amazing is that?

"Sorry, it's not in our budget. No new shoes for you." Brad shakes his head with a grin.

"Oh, I'll be getting some new heels. I'll buy them with my own hard-earned money." I wink.

"Like you need more."

"Oh, a girl always needs more shoes, Brad. You should know this by now."

"Well, all right. So then, your other stories are already turned in?"

"Correct." I nod.

The waiter comes with our food. I adore the way they present the food here. My southwest chicken wrap has flowers drawn on the plate with guacamole sauce. It's so cute. This is definitely my favorite little café. Kate and I eat here several times a week. Plus, it helps that it's right next to my apartment. It has this adorable terrace area out front with tables where we always choose to sit. It's pretty awesome that we can sit outside to eat in late November.

Brad shovels his steak salad in his mouth.

"Whoa, slow down there, boss." I laugh.

"Sorry, I have to meet Elizabeth across town in an hour. So, I have to go soon."

My face lights up with interest. "This is, like, date number...three?"

"Yeah." He nods.

"So, you like her?"

"I think so." He shrugs. "I could see dating her. So...if there's anything you want to confess...now would be the time."

He raises an eyebrow, and I can't help but laugh.

"Like my undying love for you?"

"Exactly," he says.

"Nope. Nothing to confess." I shake my head.

"Bummer."

Ever since I confronted Brad back in August, the dynamic of our relationship has changed. He still flirts on occasion, but he is always very respectful. Actually, besides Kate, he's the best friend I have here.

"So, you said the D word. Does that mean you like her for more than just a hook-up?"

"You mean, *date*?" He chuckles.

I take a sip of my iced tea. "Yeah."

"Well, we've already hooked up, and I still want to see her again, so...I suppose."

"You're such a pig."

"What? I'm just being honest."

I press my lips in a flat line. "Mmhmm."

"I'm serious here, London. If things go well, I could be off the market. You know you're still my number one. You sure you don't want to reconsider our relationship parameters?" He smirks, a salacious look in his eyes.

"Seriously, your poor mother. How did she ever give birth to someone with such a big head?"

He ignores my attempt at a joke. "Is it still the military dude?"

"His name is Loïc. And, no, not really."

"So, it's me?"

I shake my head. "No, it's not you."

"So, it's the dude then. You're not over him. Hasn't it been, like, a year?"

"Almost—at least, since I last saw him. But we technically broke up in May—or maybe, if you ask him, April through an email."

"That's real considerate of him. And you haven't spoken to him since?"

"Nope."

"London, it's time to move on. Seriously. If not with me, then with someone else. Why are you sitting around, waiting for someone who doesn't love you? You are a stunning woman. You're smart, witty, and fucking hot. You could have almost anyone you wanted."

"I'm not waiting for him. I know it's over. But I don't want anyone else—at the moment. It's fine, Brad. I'm focusing on my career and my independence right now. I don't need a man to be happy. Plus..." I start to stay before I stop myself.

"Plus what?"

I look down at my half-eaten wrap. "I don't want to be with anyone else until I can give him my whole heart, and right now, it belongs to someone else."

Brad lets out a small grunt. "This Loïc dude must be a fucking idiot."

"He's not. It's...I don't know. He was my first real love. I'm having a hard time with letting him go, I guess."

"I really hate that douche for messing you up for the rest of us," Brad huffs out.

I can't help but smile. "You'd better go. You'll be late for Elizabeth."

Brad throws a fifty down on the table and stands. "All right. Sorry to eat and run. Your stories sound great. Can't wait to see the finished versions."

"Thanks."

He starts to leave but stops when he's next to me. He bends down, and with one hand, he grabs the back of my head and leans in, pulling me into a kiss. It's short and sweet and completely unexpected.

His lips pull away from mine, but his face remains a breath away. "Anything? Did you feel anything?" he asks.

"Nope," I whisper.

"Damn," he sighs. He stands up, releasing my head. "I had to try one more time." He smiles. "Please don't come into my office and chew me out tomorrow. I promise I won't do it again." He winks.

"I won't yell at you, and you won't do it again." I smile at him, but he knows I'm serious.

"Okay. See you tomorrow, London."

"Sounds good. Give my best to Elizabeth." I grin wide.

"Will do," he says before walking away.

I take a couple of additional bites of my wrap before calling it a night, and I pay the bill. But I'm in no hurry to leave. Kate isn't home from the office yet, and it's such a gorgeous night.

I lean back in my chair and watch the people around me, the cars going by, the sun as it descends into the horizon.

Turning toward the restaurant, I catch a glimpse of myself in the storefront window. I barely recognize myself anymore. In my reflection, I see someone with strength, confidence, and happiness. All are a true testament to how far I've come. Appearing whole is quite a feat when, inside, I still feel so very broken.

Life goes on, and there is no better place to drive that sentiment home than in LA. Everything is fast-paced here. If I didn't acclimate, I'd have gotten lost.

And I realize that failing isn't an option. I need this success.

So, I move on. I adapt. I smile. Most importantly, I work hard.

And I pretend that I don't scan the faces of everyone I pass in hopes of seeing him.

You're doing okay, I tell myself. *You're doing really great.*

I have a job that I love. I haven't touched my trust fund in six months. I'm an independent woman, living a life I can be proud of. I've met some great new people.

Despite my shattered heart, I'm happy. Truthfully, I don't know if my heart will ever heal. They say that time heals all wounds, so I'm hopeful.

Goose bumps pebble across my skin.

Sometimes, when I'm thinking of Loïc, I can almost feel him. If I didn't know better, I would swear that he's here with me. I suppose, in a way, he is. They say the ones you truly love never really leave you. Though life might be easier if they did.

SIXTEEN

Loïc

"I never thought I'd see the day when I thought someone's spit was adorable."
—Loïc Berkeley

"Oh my gosh! Look at him in this Santa hat, Loïc," Sarah says to me before saying to Evan in a baby voice, "You got the chubby cheeks. Yes, you do. You're the chubbiest and the cutest."

"He's pretty damn cute," I agree.

Evan will be four months old tomorrow, and he really is a beautiful baby. His wrist and ankle rolls along with his double chin that loves to collect drool just add to his cuteness. He smiles all the time and has just started laughing, which might be my favorite sound in the world.

"It's your first Christmas, and you are the cutest Santa baby Mommy ever did see," Sarah coos.

She bounces Evan on her knee, and he belly-laughs in his Santa romper.

Life in the Berkeley home is pretty great. Sarah hasn't gone back to work yet. I told her to stay home and be with Evan for as long as she wants. The house is paid off, and our bills are minimal. There's no reason for her to miss out on time with Evan. He's growing so fast, and I want her to be able to experience all of it.

She's an amazing mom, just like I knew she would be. I know she wants to give Evan everything that she didn't have, and she's already doing a great job. Maggie and her family have adopted Sarah and Evan as their own as well. He is one loved little boy. There's just something about a baby that mends broken hearts.

Each week, I continue to go to multiple types of therapy—individual and support groups. I've even started to lead some of the group sessions. I feel pretty good now, but I know it's because of the medication I'm on and all the therapy. I'm always going to be someone with PTSD. It will get more manageable over time, but it'll always be there. I'm fortunate that I got help before it dragged me too far down. Eventually, I hope to be well enough to help other veterans get the help they need.

"What a great Christmas. I love our little family!" Sarah exclaims as she snaps some photos of Evan.

"Do you want to see if he can open one of his presents?" I ask her.

"Sure." She sets Evan on her lap and puts a box in front of him. "Here you go, buddy. Like this." She demonstrates how to rip off the paper.

Evan gurgles and coos and drops a glob of drool on top of the box, but he doesn't do much more. I never thought I'd see the day when I thought someone's spit was adorable.

"Look, bud. See? Like this." I slowly rip the paper off of his wrapped toy. "Rip the paper. Rip the paper," I chant in a silly voice.

Evan giggles and flails his arms. He hits the present, but I think it was just because it was in his way.

"He'll get it next year," I say to Sarah with a chuckle.

"Yeah. More for us to unwrap, I guess." She grins. "Here, let's take a family selfie."

I position myself close to her. She holds her cell phone out and takes a photo of the three of us. Evan even smiles for it, but he's always smiling.

"Aw, that's a total framer," she says, admiring the photo.

After opening presents, we eat the delicious cinnamon rolls that Sarah made, and then she heads to Evan's room to put him down for his first nap of the day.

I make quick calls to Maggie, Cooper's family, and Dixon.

I reached out to him back in July when I decided to get some help. He's become a real friend, calling and checking in with me a couple of times a week.

"He was tired," Sarah says, entering the room. "Being so precious is exhausting."

She plops down next to me on the sofa. "I love you," she says, leaning her head against my shoulder with a happy sigh.

"I love you, too."

"Marry me, Loïc."

My body freezes. "Sarah," I say on an exhale.

"I know, I know." She sits up to look at me. "We're family. You love me like a sister. Blah, blah, blah. I know." She lets out a frustrated groan. "But it could be so much more, if you'd just try."

"Sarah…"

ELLIE WADE

"No, listen to me. We live together. We're raising the most amazing little boy together. We've each seen the other at their worst and loved them anyway. No one loves me like you do, Loïc, and no one will ever love or understand you the way I do. You see me as a sister because that's what you allow yourself to see. Just try seeing me another way. Try opening your heart up for more. Just try." Her big blue eyes stare into mine, pleading.

Closing my eyes, I bring my hand to my forehead and rub my temple, thinking. If things were different and there had never been a London, then…*maybe*. Perhaps I could have learned to love Sarah differently.

But London did happen, and now, I know what it feels like to be truly in love with someone else.

"I can't do that to you." I hold Sarah's hands in mine. "I love you, Sarah…so much. I would do anything for you; you know that. But I can't take away your chance at real love. I will never love you in the way a husband should love his wife. I could fake it, but that wouldn't be fair to either of us. You're a beautiful, wonderful woman with so much to offer. You deserve your happily ever after. I won't take that away from you. You'll find it. I promise."

"But I already have my fairy tale. You and Evan are my life. I don't want anything else." Her voice quivers.

"If you think that, it's because you've never truly been in love. I have, and I know the difference."

"If life was so great with London, then why aren't you with her now? If it were true love, then it would have lasted, Loïc. The longest-lasting relationship in your life is me." She points her finger toward her chest. "I'm the one for you. Me."

"I'm sorry," I say softly.

"Why are you so stubborn?" she yells. "Why can't you see what you have?"

"What do you want me to do here?" I groan.

"I want you to marry me. I want to be a real family."

"We are a family already. I will always be Evan's uncle. I will always be here for you, but I can't love you like that, Sarah. I can't."

Sarah stands. "God, I hate you!" she cries.

I rise from the couch and pull her into my arms as she cries. "I wish I could give you more. I'm sorry."

"Eventually, you'll see. You'll realize." She sniffles into my chest.

If there were never a London, lots of things would be different. But London happened, and there isn't a damn thing I can do to pretend she didn't.

SEVENTEEN

London

Eight Months Later

*"I don't care about yesterday.
All I want is tomorrow and the day after that."*
—London Wright

I'm putting the finishing touches on my mascara when Kate pops her head in the bathroom.

"I thought you had this weekend off?"

"I was supposed to. The new girl, Ginger, was supposed to be covering this story. But, apparently, she flaked out and set sail on a booze cruise for the weekend."

"What's a booze cruise?" Kate asks.

I laugh. "Exactly what it sounds like—a cruise ship with lots of drinking."

"And she just ditched her story?"

"Well, when Brad hires a woman just because he wants to sleep with her...what do you expect?" I roll my eyes.

"So, she's not the best employee?"

"Hardly," I scoff with a shake of my head.

"Well, he hired you because he wanted to sleep with you," she reminds me.

"Obviously, I'm the exception to the rule." I chuckle. "Anyway, he called and begged me to cover it. I shouldn't be long. I'll be back before dinner. Did you still want to try that new sushi place?"

Kate follows me to my room. "Yes, definitely. I have a book I'm dying to finish anyway, so I'm going to veg all day and read."

I throw on a sundress. "Sounds like a perfect Saturday to me. Are you still reading that one without the HEA?"

"No. I finished that one."

"I still can't believe you read it, knowing he was going to die." I lean down to buckle my sandals.

"I know. It was brutal, but it had, like, almost all five stars. So, I had to see what all the fuss was about."

"Is the one you're reading a cliffy?"

Kate shakes her head. "It'd better not be. It's a stand-alone."

"My heart hasn't healed from the last book you lent me." I dramatically clutch my heart to prove my point.

"I know, but it was, like, the best book hangover ever, right?"

"Oh, totally." I grin, grabbing my purse and cell phone. "Let's pick back up on our *Grey's Anatomy* marathon tonight."

"I can't," Kate says. "My heart can't take it. Denny died, London. Ugh, too sad."

"I know, but sometimes, it's nice to have a good cry, isn't it?"

I head toward the door, and Kate follows.

"Um, no. It's sad," she disagrees.

"Yeah, right. That's why you just read a book where you knew the hero would die. Admit it. It's cathartic to cry your eyes out every now and then."

"Whatever." She chuckles.

"All right, I'm out. *Grey's* and sushi tonight. It's a date."

I find a seat in the auditorium and scroll through my phone. I read the email Brad sent me, making sure I understand the essence of what he wants for the article.

The talk is being run by a group of veterans who travel around the country, trying to bring light to current issues regarding veterans and some of the obstacles they face when they return from war.

I pull my laptop out and open it up. I've tried taking notes on my phone, an iPad, and with straight-up pen and paper. But I've found that typing out my notes is the easiest for me. I set up my recorder as well, which is always handy if I need to go back and listen to something again.

A colonel who served in Vietnam comes out first. He's wearing the Purple Heart he received from the President of the United States for his acts of bravery during the war. The colonel takes a seat in the center of the stage and tells the crowd about a specific mission where over two hundred men went in but only forty-four men survived. His job was to fly a helicopter through enemy fire to rescue the injured men.

I'm glad I'm recording his speech because it's so interesting that I'm having a hard time typing out notes.

When he finishes, he receives a standing ovation.

I close my laptop and put it back in my purse. I can tell this is going to be so fascinating that I'm going to have to just listen again and take notes from the recording later.

I lift my head after situating my purse to see the next soldier walking out onstage. I gasp loudly as I grab ahold of the armrests of the chair, hoping the contact will center me.

There *he* stands, after all this time. My heart beats loudly in my chest, so boldly that I can hear the drumming resonating throughout my body. Or maybe I can't hear it at all over the piercing hum screeching from my ears. I don't know what I hear or feel. I can't focus. I can't think.

I suck in jagged raw breaths. My body's acute awareness of him brings a torrent of emotions, making it hard for me to find oxygen. The sorrow that courses through me burns with a tangible pain.

There he is…

Loïc.

A flood of warm tears streams down my face, falling onto my lap. I've completely lost the ability to control my body's reaction to seeing Loïc for the first time in so long—twenty months, to be exact.

I know exactly how long it's been since I've seen his face. I know because not a day goes by when I don't think of him, mourn for him, and miss him. Not a night goes by when I don't dream of him. Not a second goes by when I don't love him.

The rush of blood coursing through my body subsides enough that the ringing in my ears quiets so that I can hear his words as he speaks.

"The problem with PTSD and depression is that, for many soldiers, they don't know how bad it is until it's too late. Those who go into the armed forces have a certain type of mentality. Soldiers are strong, tough, resilient. Men and women go into the military because they think they have what it takes to defend our country, to go to war, to fight.

"But it doesn't matter how strong someone is. Some things are so gruesome that our brains can't process them. Humans are not meant to kill other humans. Taking another's life is something that's impossible to forget. Watching another soldier be tortured or killed isn't something you can get over. Watching your best friend be blown into little pieces isn't something you can get over."

Loïc pauses. He looks down toward the ground. His chest rises as he pulls in air.

Then, he continues with renewed conviction, "Yes, many soldiers come home, but they never come home the same. Even if they aren't physically damaged, they are mentally wounded. There's such a stigma regarding mental illness in this country that many soldiers don't seek the help they need. There's shame that comes with admitting that you're mentally unwell. So, many soldiers choose to suffer alone, believing that they'll be able to pull themselves out of the hole. Yet, before they know it, the darkness takes over and pulls them under.

"Twenty-two veterans commit suicide every single day. Twenty-two." Loïc's voice breaks with the last word. He scans the crowd.

Raw emotion prickles across my skin as my heart threatens to beat out of my chest with its inexplicable pull toward him.

Loïc continues, "That number is unacceptable. We are failing our soldiers. The mental demons that accompany many soldiers home can lead to depression, rage, substance abuse, addiction, and mental illness. It is estimated that two hundred thousand veterans are homeless on any given day. Two hundred thousand." He breaks off again, allowing the number to sink in.

"These are people who put their lives on the line to serve our country. They are someone's sister, brother, son, daughter, husband, wife, or friend, and we are failing them. We have to bring more awareness to the battles our veterans fight when they come home. More resources need to be available for them. We owe it to them to help when they can't help themselves. These are good people who gave up everything for their country."

It is with a near tangible sorrow that Loïc says, "I've been there. I've seen the darkness, and I know how lonely it is."

A frenzy of emotions pounds through my veins, the loudest being guilt.

Loïc pulls in a steady breath before going on, "I lost so much, yet I'm one of the lucky ones because I'm standing here before you today. We need to stand together to help our soldiers. Thank you."

The crowd rises to clap for Loïc.

I can't make myself stand. My legs feel shaky and weak. I didn't hear the beginning of Loïc's speech, and I could barely comprehend the latter part. But I heard enough.

I heard enough to know the horror he must have been going through.

Loïc was drowning in a dark depression, and I left him. I should have known. It didn't make any sense. I tried to respect him by giving him what he wanted. Yet he didn't have a clue what he wanted because he needed help.

Why didn't I fight harder?

The guilt that floods my mind weighs down on me like a tsunami of despair, threatening to drown me in remorse.

The worst part is, I can't go back. I can't change any of it. I wasn't there for Loïc when he needed me the most, and there's nothing I can do about it.

I'm so ashamed.

I left him.

I left the love of my life when he needed me.

But I didn't know.

That thought brings me no absolution from my guilt. None.

I pull in air, but it doesn't reach my lungs. I inhale again and again.

I feel faint.

I have to get out of here.

Standing, I throw the recorder into my purse.

"Excuse me. Excuse me," I say to those I pass as I get closer to the aisle.

Once I'm in the clear, I run toward the back exit of the auditorium. A desperate desire to escape this room propels me. I throw the door open and sprint across the lobby toward the entry doors.

Outside, I stumble toward the side of the building, thankful it's shaded from the hot California sun. My back against the building's brick exterior, I crumble to the ground in a heap of sobs.

In an instant, the strong, independent woman I've worked so hard to be dissolves, and I'm just a heartbroken girl, crying for everything she's lost.

Seeing Loïc up on that stage—the real standing, breathing, talking Loïc—is something I can't wrap my mind around. Since he left, I'd simply close my eyes, and he would be there. He never truly left me. Yet seeing him in the flesh is more powerful than I can handle.

"London?"

I lift my face from my knees and quickly scramble to my feet, hastily wiping under my eyes. I take in a few calming breaths.

"I thought I saw you leaving the auditorium. I can't believe it's…you." He stumbles on his words.

He's here, right in front of me. My love. My Loïc.

I love him. God, I love him.

I've missed him with a tangible ache every single minute since he left that December morning, twenty months ago.

His deep blue eyes scan me from my feet to my head as I simultaneously take stock of him. He looks the same yet so different somehow. I notice some scarring on his right arm and the side of his neck. There's some evidence of old wounds on the side of his cheek, but someone who hadn't known Loïc before, the way I did, wouldn't even notice them.

But I know every inch of his skin. Memories of Loïc have kept me going for so long. I've imagined running my palm along his cheek and down his chest—just feeling his warmth in every way possible—every day since he left. My dreams of him, both when I'm awake and asleep, have sustained my aching heart.

I've loved every part of Loïc. I still do.

"Hi," I say weakly. There are so many things I want to tell him, and now is my chance, but I don't even know where to start.

"Hi." He grins, and my heart nearly falls out of my chest.

His smile is genuinely happy. His eyes shine with what seems to be joy to see me. He's in his military uniform, and he is truly the most beautiful man I've ever seen.

It's reminiscent of the first time I saw him in uniform at the charity car wash, which seems like a lifetime ago. Except I can tell he's not the same man who pulled up in that dirty truck way back then. I'm nowhere near the same girl I was then either.

"How are you?" he asks.

I let out a forced laugh as my hand gestures from my head to my feet. "I've obviously been better."

I can't take it anymore. His proximity is maddening.

"Can I please hug you?" I blurt out.

"Yeah."

He takes a step toward me, and I throw my arms around him.

Being in physical contact with Loïc again sends my senses into overdrive. It's completely overwhelming. My tears start falling again, and there's no hope in stopping them. So, I let them fall onto Loïc's uniform, and I hug him tighter.

"I'm so sorry," he whispers into my hair. His arms pull me in tighter.

"I'm sorry," I sob into his chest. "I'm so sorry."

The two of us stand in this embrace for some time. I'm in no hurry to release him because I don't know if I'll ever get to hold him again. I'm committing the feeling of his body against mine to memory.

Eventually, when my tears have run dry, I drop my arms and take a step back.

"I don't know what to say," I admit, my entire body feeling tired and heavy.

With a thoughtful expression, he asks, "Are you happy?"

"Yeah. Are you?"

"I am." He nods.

"Well, that's...great," I offer. The simple sight of Loïc before me makes my knees weak.

"What are you doing here? Did you know I'd be here?"

I shake my head with a sad chuckle. "Uh, no. Hence, this mess." I point to myself. "I was assigned to write an article about this." I bite my lip. "Well, crap. I guess the story is just going to be about you and the guy before you."

Pulling his shoulders back, he smiles. "I'm proud of you, London."

I grab the base of my neck, rubbing out the tension. "For what?"

"For coming out here and living your dream, being a fancy journalist."

I sigh, dropping my arm to my side. "Well, I have you to thank for that." I shake my head. "I'm sorry. I didn't mean..."

"It's fine. I know." He nods slowly.

I swallow hard. "I didn't want to leave you, Loïc. I would have done anything for you."

"I know, and I'm sorry I pushed you away. I was in a very dark place. I wasn't thinking clearly. In my mind at the time, I thought you'd be better off without me. It was a cowardly move, but it was all I was capable of then."

"Are you feeling better?"

"Yeah, I am. I got help. Lots of doctors, medications. I've been able to get off most of my medications, but I'll always have to stay on top of my mental health. It will probably be an ongoing struggle. But talking to others, like I did today, is very therapeutic."

"I'm so glad you're better, Loïc. How are Sarah and the baby?" I ask with a clench of my jaw.

"Great. Evan's first birthday is next week. He's the most adorable little boy. I love him so much."

"I'm happy for you," I say even though my heart is shattering all over again as I think of Loïc with Sarah and their beautiful little family.

"How's your boyfriend?" Loïc's question seems random.

My eyes dart up to his. "Uh, I don't have one."

"You broke up?" he inquires.

"I haven't dated anyone since you, Loïc." For some reason, I want him to know that.

A mixture of emotions crosses his face, the most obvious being confusion. "But I saw you."

"What do you mean?" I bite my lip with a frown.

"Last year, I flew out here to see you. I got your address from Maggie. I went to your apartment and saw you sitting outside on a restaurant patio, right next to your place. There was a man, and he kissed you. I didn't want to ruin anything for you. So, after seeing that you were happy, I just left."

I hold my hands to my sides as they start to tremble. "What?" I shriek, barely able to process his words. "You came for me?" My eyes fill with tears once more.

Disappointment gleams in his eyes. "Yeah, but you were happy...and..."

"And nothing. I wasn't happy without you. I certainly wasn't dating anyone. That was my boss, and he kissed me to be funny. That was the second and last time he ever kissed me. I can't believe you came out here, and you didn't come see me." My voice rises. I gulp down the ache that's building a tightness in my throat.

"I was going to, but I told myself, if you were happy, then I would leave you alone. You looked great, London. I didn't want to bring you pain."

"I can't believe this." I shake my head. "I just can't. So, you're with Sarah now?"

"No, I'm not with her."

"You're not?" I ask, my voice shaky. "What about the baby?"

"I love Evan, of course, but I'm his uncle, not his dad."

The weight in my chest lessens. "Are you dating anyone?"

He shakes his head. "No, not since you."

I pause, pulling in a long breath. I nervously search his eyes as I ask, "Do you still love me, Loïc?" My voice trembles, and my heartbeat quickens. My lips part to accommodate faster breaths.

He lifts his arm and gently pulls a strand of my hair between his fingers. "Every minute of every day."

I press my quivering lips together, afraid to speak. I've hoped and prayed that this day would come, that I would hear Loïc tell me he loves me. Now that it has, I'm so overcome with emotions that I could just crumble.

"I'm going to kiss you now," he says, his deep timbre thick with love, desire, and need.

Before I can think straight, his full lips are crashing on mine, desperate and intense. My skewed equilibrium causes me to sway. I grip his back with my trembling hands, holding me upright. He ravishes my mouth with his.

Something innate takes over as a torrent of emotions fall down on me. I kiss him back with a fiery need.

Our lips collide. Our tongues dance. Our souls reconnect.

This is the greatest instant of my life.

Loïc's hypnotic spell of a kiss mends my heart in a way that time never could. Nothing matters but this moment right now, today. This kiss communicates so much, but what I hear the most is the hope for tomorrow.

All I've ever wanted with Loïc is a future. I don't care about yesterday. All I want is tomorrow and the day after that. And just maybe I'll be gifted with enough tomorrows to last a lifetime.

I begrudgingly pull away from our kiss. "I realize that I have a major flaw."

"Oh, yeah? What's that?" Loïc asks, his voice husky.

"My heart's incapable of loving anyone but you," I admit, a small smile forming.

Loïc pulls in a sharp breath before saying, "I'm flawed in the same way. My heart only beats for you, London Wright. No one else."

And then his lips find mine once more.

EIGHTEEN

Loïc

"I don't know what I did to deserve her love,
but I'm never going to deny myself again."
—Loïc Berkeley

I sneak a peek over to London at the same time she takes her eyes off the road to glance at me. Our eyes meet briefly before she turns back to the road with a giggle.

"This is awkward, right?" she asks from the driver's seat.

"A little," I agree.

"But amazing, too?"

"Definitely." I smile.

"When's your return flight?"

"Tomorrow morning, eight o'clock."

London sighs, "Uh, that sucks."

"Yeah," I agree.

She parks on the street in front of her apartment building. I think back to last year when I saw her sitting at that restaurant with that guy in his expensive suit. She was laughing and smiling. She looked stunning, and when he kissed her, I had to go. If I had only known, the past year would have been so different.

We both exit her car and meet on the sidewalk. London reaches out her hand, and I entwine my fingers through hers. Just the feeling of her hand in mine does crazy things to me. This day has been so surreal.

"I can't wait for you to see our apartment," she says as we walk into the building and up the stairs. "Kate and I redecorated the entire thing. When I moved in, every room was painted a different bright color—yellow, green, red. I'm talking, like, neon shades. It was hideous. Kate and I spent weeks finding stuff at flea markets and secondhand stores. We painted the entire place by ourselves."

"You painted?" I ask with a quirk of my eyebrow.

"Yep. I guess I've changed a lot since the last time I saw you."

"I suppose we both have," I agree.

"Yeah," she says quietly.

She opens a door on the second floor and pulls me in with her.

"Oh, praise Jesus. I'm dying of hunger in here," a peppy Southern accent says. A girl about London's age with wavy bright red hair enters the living room. "Oh, hey." She stops in her tracks when she sees me.

"I ran into someone today," London says. "Kate, this is Loïc. Loïc, my roommate, Kate," she says by way of introduction.

"*The* Loïc?" Kate asks, her voice rising an octave.

"Yep," London answers.

"Nice to meet you." I extend my hand toward Kate, and she shakes it.

"You, too. Oh, wow. Well, I'll let y'all catch up and stuff. I'm going to head out and get dinner, I think."

"It's okay. We're starving, too," London tells Kate. "Does sushi sound okay?" she asks me.

"Sounds great."

"All right, let me just go fix this mess"—she motions toward her face—"and we'll head out."

She's cried off all of her makeup, and her eyes are slightly red and puffy.

And she's the most beautiful woman I've ever seen.

I take a bite of my seaweed salad as Kate talks about her big move from Mississippi to LA. She's a chatty little thing, which I like because it gives me lots of time to stare at London. God, I've missed her. I don't know what's going to happen after today, but I know I can't go back to life without her, not after seeing her again.

"What about you, Loïc? What's life like in Michigan?" Kate asks.

"Well, I'm involved in a lot of groups at the VA hospital."

"What's the VA?" Kate wonders.

"It stands for Veterans Administration. It's a hospital for veterans."

"Oh, I see." She nods in understanding.

"Anyway, I run some groups there, mainly for PTSD. I travel around, giving talks—like the one I did today—to raise awareness for issues that affect our veterans. So, I keep myself busy. But I'm retired or honorably medically discharged. I've been thinking about going back to college for something else. But I haven't had time so far. I live with my sister and little nephew. He's almost one."

"I didn't know you had a sister," Kate says.

"Well, she's not technically my sister, but she's the closest thing to it." I sneak a glance at London, knowing there's some animosity between her and Sarah. If it's bothering her that I'm talking about Sarah, it doesn't show.

"So, what do you two spend your days doing?" I ask.

"Well, Kate and I work together. She's the receptionist for our office. We read, shop, watch marathons of TV shows. Nothing too exciting. I work a lot," London says.

I can't help but smile when London speaks about her life out here. I've always been extremely attracted to London, but seeing her so independent and successful just boosts my attraction to her up a notch.

Back at London's apartment, Kate excuses herself to go read, and London and I find our way to her bedroom.

She closes the door behind herself and kicks off her sandals. "Are you comfortable in your uniform?"

"Yeah." I nod.

"All right." She shrugs and lies across her bed on her side.

She pats the other side of the mattress. I grin before lying down across from her.

We face each other like two bookends with an untold story between us.

"Where do we go from here?" she asks.

"I don't want to be with anyone else, London."

"Me either." Her voice quivers. "I've missed you so much."

"Me, too." I lean in for a soft kiss. "London, I feel like I owe you an explanation for my behavior."

"You don't have to, if it's too hard," she offers me an out.

"No, I do because you have to know that it was never you. You hold no blame in this. You are and always have been perfect to me." I tuck an errant lock of her hair behind her ear.

I don't know where to start or what to say. So, I start with Cooper, and I tell her the truth—every ugly bit of it. She listens attentively as I talk about our mission, the grenade, Cooper's death, and waking up in Germany without my leg.

London gasps. "You lost your leg?" She looks down toward my legs, covered in my fatigues.

It startles me that she didn't know. But how could she? I walk without a limp now, and my leg's covered.

Suddenly, I'm very self-conscious and filled with doubt.

London looks back up to my face. "You know I don't care, Loïc. Right? You're not worried about that, are you?"

"Maybe a little," I admit.

London starts to cry and wraps her arms around me, burying her face against my chest. "Is that why you wouldn't let me see you?"

"Partly, but it wasn't just the leg. It was the depression and the posttraumatic stress. I wasn't well. I felt useless, unworthy, guilty, and utterly hopeless. At the time, I thought you deserved better. I thought I was doing the right thing by breaking it off. I didn't have the courage to do it in person because I knew you'd find a way to talk me out of it. I didn't want to be talked out of it because I was convinced that, down the road, you would leave me for someone else, someone whole in every way. I was just…a vacant shell. I was hurting so much, and I knew I couldn't survive you leaving me. So, I ended it on my terms. You have to understand that I wasn't thinking clearly, but in that moment, I thought I was doing you a favor."

"Loïc, that's not how real love works. Would you ever leave me if I were sick or hurt?"

"No."

"Then, why did you think I could have done that to you? I love you, Loïc. *Love you*," she says, emphasizing the last words. "Nothing in this world could make me stop. Heck, I've been trying to get over you for over a year now, and I love you more than ever." She peppers light kisses across my face.

She continues speaking, "I don't know why we work, but we do. On the outside, looking in, it appears that we have nothing in common. We're complete opposites in almost every way. We come from different backgrounds. But none of that matters. All I know is that my soul craves yours. My heart needs yours. My mind loves yours."

"I love you, too, London. So much. I'm so sorry that I put you through so much heartache but know that I never meant to. I came for you as soon as I was able. I'm sorry I misread the situation. I could have saved us a lot of heartache." I run my hand down her back.

"I hated our time apart, but maybe we needed it. It gave me some time to work on some of my flaws," she says.

"Me, too. Though I love all of your flaws," I admit truthfully.

"Well, I hope you have a few less to love now." She winks. "I feel like I'm a better version of myself. I think we've both been trying to become a person the other could be proud of."

"I was always proud of you," I say.

"As I was of you, but now, we're both walking with our heads held high. We're proud of ourselves. That's kinda great, you know?"

I nod. "Yeah, I think I do."

"Now that I've got you back, I'm never going to let you go." She smiles, and another small tear rolls down her cheek.

"I'm going to hold you to that." I let out a sigh. "'Cause, you see, London, I'm always going to be imperfect in more ways than one."

"And I'm going to love you, imperfections and all, for the rest of my life."

I don't know who leans in first, but our lips find each other, and we kiss again. The kiss is smooth and sweet. It's packed with love and loss, desperation and hope. I can taste the saltiness of London's tears as my mouth continues to move against hers.

I've never loved anyone as much as I love her, and I know I never will.

Maybe she's right. This time apart has made us into better versions of ourselves so that we can truly give each other everything we have.

The kiss goes on for so long that it's all I feel. Every ounce of energy I have is put into it.

Breaths. Tongues. Lips. Desire.

I worship this woman. I don't know what I did to deserve her love, but I'm never going to deny myself again.

London pulls away. My mouth is cold without hers.

"I need you, Loïc."

My muscles tighten with her words. I want to be inside her more than anything. Yet, in order to do that, I'm going to have to face a deep fear.

London senses my hesitation. She kisses me on the forehead and rolls away from me. She gets off the bed and walks around it. "Sit up, please," she says sweetly.

I do as she asked. I sit on the edge of the bed, my feet touching the ground, and I face her. I watch in amazement as she unzips the back of her sundress and lets it fall to the floor. With one flick of her hand behind her back, her bra joins the dress. Finally, she steps out of her panties.

"This is me, all of me, wanting all of you." She takes a step toward me.

I reach my hands out and hold her hips. Pulling her against me, I rub my nose along her stomach.

"You're so soft," I say as my hands glide up and down her satin skin.

"Let me help you, Loïc," she says as she starts to unbutton my shirt.

My heart accelerates. My body is a ball of nerves.

She pulls off my shirt and then my undershirt, leaving my chest bare. Her hands roam down to loosen my belt buckle and then my pants.

"Lean back, Loïc," she whispers.

I do as she said.

She grabs ahold of my pants and boxers and begins to shimmy them down my hips. I feel the fabric move down my pelvis and to my thighs, and I hold my breath as she pulls them past my knee and to my ankles.

My heart beats so wildly beneath my chest that I'm sure she can hear it. I'm lying here, naked and exposed.

"Can you take it off?" She nervously searches my eyes, motioning toward the metal leg.

"I don't have to."

"I want you to," she pleads gently.

I pull off my prosthesis and let it drop to the ground.

London's bottom lip starts to tremble as her eyes fill with tears once more. Her beautiful brown gaze finds mine, and she holds us there—in this quiet space where no words are spoken, but so much is said.

She guides her hands down my face, my arms, and my chest, healing me with her touch. Her fingertip traces each scar before she kisses it. She supplies extra kisses to the scar on my side where I was hit with a large piece of shrapnel.

Finally, she makes her way down to my leg. Her fingertip presses lightly against the scarred skin, tracing the web of healed cuts and the outline of staples and stitches still present across the marred skin.

Her eyes, wide with adoration and pride, lift to mine. Her lips part as she breathes in, her breath steady. The love she shines on me is unwavering.

Breaking our stare, she drops her attention back to my leg where she proceeds to place soft kisses against every inch of the damaged stump. I suck in air. Raw and ragged breaths carry much-needed oxygen to my brain. Grabbing at the sheets on either side of me, I attempt to ground myself. London's emphatic pronouncement, her kisses of unrelenting love, sears me to the core.

"Loïc, don't ever be ashamed of your scars." Tears fall down her cheeks. "Your scars are proof of the battles you've fought and survived. You could have checked out completely, but you didn't. You fought to come back. You fought to live. You fought when your heart felt it

167

had nothing to fight for. You are strong. You are brave. You are a warrior. And don't you ever forget it."

My eyes fill with unshed tears as this moment with London is more than I could have ever asked for. She's not looking at me like I'm wounded. She's looking at me like I'm powerful.

Her tongue darts out to lick her lips. Her trembling skin is flushed as her dilated pupils stare at me.

In her face, I see a myriad of emotions—love, respect, and pride, to name a few—but the one I love most of all is lust. Even though I'm broken, she desires me every bit as much as I do her.

She places me at her entrance, and as she slides down, we let out a collective moan of pleasure because London and I together is the greatest feeling in the world.

Utter fucking perfection.

"Oh my God," London cries into the heated space. Her hips move eagerly up and down against me, her internal wall squeezing me.

My shaky hands move over every inch of her skin, ravishing it, burning it with my touch. I need to feel London, all of her.

"Oh my God," London says again with a shaky inhalation as she falls on top of my chest in a heap of tears.

"It's okay," I whisper, dragging my fingertips up her back.

This moment carries an incredible ache with a vast contradiction of emotions. I understand what London's feeling because I feel it, too.

How does one grasp the moment when a heart once thought to be broken for eternity heals?

I flip us so that London is lying on the bed beneath me. Pressing my forearms into the mattress on either side of her head, boxing her in with my arms, I kiss her. I slowly pepper soft kisses across her cheeks, tasting the saltiness of her tears.

After I kiss the tip of her nose, I say, "I know...this is so incredible that it hurts, but I promise that this will be the last time I ever cause you pain, London."

I start to move into London again. With each unhurried push, I place my lips against hers.

"I. Love. You," I say, each word staccato. "I'm never leaving you again. I promise. Okay?"

London nods as her hands grab my face. Our lips collide in a crash of insane desire. With each rhythmic movement against each other, our cadence accelerates. Our need intensifies.

London continues to kiss me senseless, our tongues licking greedily.

The rest of the world has fallen away, and it's just me and London, together, in this perfect moment filled with kisses, promises, and an intense amount of love.

I move faster, bringing London closer to the edge. She pants wildly, digging her fingers into my back.

"Loïc," she whimpers from the back of her throat. Her eyes become unfocused before her lids close.

I steel myself for the release to come, rocking myself into London at the angle I know she craves. It's been so long, but I know her body, every bit of it. I know what she needs.

London yells with a half-sob as she begins to shudder beneath me, waves of ecstasy erupting through her body. I follow her, groaning with enormous jolts of pleasure.

I cradle my face into London's neck, feeling the blood rushing through her veins against my cheek.

"I love you so much," I declare over and over against her skin.

"I love you." She holds me tight. "More than you could ever know. Thank you for coming back to me."

London never fails to make my heart still.

NINETEEN

London

> *"For the first time in a very long time, I have no regrets, and my soul is completely at peace."*
> —London Wright

My legs drape over Loïc's as we sit in the airport. I probably look needy and clingy, but I just can't stop touching him.

"Here's a red." I place a red gummy bear, Loïc's favorite flavor, in his mouth.

"Thanks, babe." He chews the gummy. "I still think it's awesome that your boss gave you a four-day weekend."

"Please," I scoff. "I work my ass off for him. He'd better. Plus, I turned in all of my articles, so there wasn't a reason for him to say no. I can't wait to surprise Paige." I grin.

Paige has been out to visit me a handful of times, but I haven't been back to Michigan since I left.

"I can't wait to see her either. I adore her."

"Yeah," I agree. "She's a keeper."

I lean in and give Loïc a kiss. "Thank you for missing your flight and spending the week with me," I whisper against his lips.

"Oh, you've thanked me. Many times." A rumbly chuckle vibrates through his chest.

"I've missed us. All of us. But especially *that* part." I give him a wink.

"Yeah, that part's pretty great," he concurs.

"Have you gotten ahold of Sarah?"

"Yeah, I told her I was bringing someone back from Cali and to add one more to the guest list for Evan's party."

"No, you have to tell her it's me. She hates me. She needs to know that I'm coming, so she can prepare herself."

"She doesn't hate you. And who else would I be bringing back from LA?"

"You didn't see her out on the porch that day I came to your house. She didn't want me anywhere around you. I know you told her that you didn't want to see me, but she took great joy in delivering the message. Trust me." I roll my eyes. "Honestly, I would have bet money that you two were married by now. I was sure she'd won you over."

Loïc laughs. "Well, she definitely tried."

"I knew it! What happened?"

"Don't hold it against her, London. I'm the only stable man she's known in her life. I'm the only man who's loved her. She just wants to be happy. You can't blame her. Someday, she'll fall in love with someone for real, and then she'll understand that not all love is equal."

"Were you two ever together?" I ask timidly.

"No." He shakes his head. "No one else since you."

I exhale a breath of relief. "And it's not weird, living with her?"

"No. I mean, we've had a couple of awkward moments, but they always pass. It's been great. I've loved helping with Evan. And I know you're not a fan of Sarah, but please try. She's very special to me, and she'll always be in my life."

"Huh. I'll try if she tries." I cross my arms over my chest.

"There's the London I know and love," Loïc kids with a chuckle. He says in a serious tone, "I know she's not your favorite person, but she really helped me get through everything."

"I would have helped you if you had let me," I grumble.

"I know." Loïc grins. "Come here. I need your lips."

We kiss like two PDA-obsessed teenagers, and I couldn't care less. The gate attendant calls our flight for boarding.

"Do you remember the first time we were on a plane together?" I ask Loïc with a smirk.

Loïc grabs our carry-ons, and we line up. "Sure do. I was coming back from drill. Louisville, Kentucky."

"Seems like so long ago," I say thoughtfully.

"I remember how badly you wanted me back then. Ah, and your Twenty Questions game. God, I was kinda an ass, too, wasn't I?" Loïc strings random thoughts together, obviously replaying that flight in his head.

I laugh. "A little bit, but it just made me want you more. And, yeah…I wanted you, but you're the one who kissed me, so you wanted me, too."

"Maybe I did. Maybe I didn't." He grins down at me.

"Oh, you did."
He did.

It seems so weird to be driving up to Loïc's house. So much has happened since the last time I stepped foot inside this place. Most notably, Cooper's death. The house isn't going to seem the same without Cooper making it smell amazing with his cooking skills.

Yet the first thing that surprises me when we walk in is how good it smells. Loïc holds my hand and leads me to the kitchen, and I almost expect to see Cooper standing there, but instead, it's her.

She has her back to us. Her blonde hair is up in a messy bun. A pink apron is tied around her tiny waist as she stirs something inside a bowl while her hips move from side to side to the music playing from the speakers.

"Hey. We're home," Loïc says quietly so that he won't startle her.

She jumps anyway before reaching for the speakers and turning down the music. "Hey!" she says cheerfully to Loïc.

I watch her gaze trail from Loïc to me and then down to our entwined hands.

"Well, looks like you had quite the trip. I'd ask if it was a good one, but I can see that it was. Hi, London. How are you?" She smiles, and it almost looks sincere.

"Good. How are you?"

"Just great. Getting the food prepped for the party tomorrow."

"Oh, where's the baby?" I ask excitedly right about the time I notice the Pack 'N Play in the corner of the kitchen.

A little blond cherub is standing up, holding the side of the playpen. He's now shaking it back and forth, saying, "Yo, Yo, Yo."

"Hey, buddy." Loïc picks him and swoops him through the air with airplane sounds while Evan giggles. "Ev, I want you to meet someone really special." Loïc holds baby Evan at his side. "Can you say *London*?"

"Yo!" Evan calls out.

"Yes, Yo's home, buddy," Loïc says to the baby. He turns to me. "He can't say his Ls or make the *ick* sound, so my name comes out as Yo."

"Aw, that's adorable. You make a cute Uncle Yo." I reach out toward Evan, and he grabs my finger and shakes it. "Aren't you just the cutest?" I say to him.

I turn to see Sarah watching us. "What's on the menu for tomorrow?" I ask her.

"Um, let's see. Grilled barbeque chicken, cheesy hash-brown casserole, homemade coleslaw, a ginger poppy-seed salad, some finger-food type stuff, and of course, the cake."

"Oh, wow. You're making all of that yourself?" I ask, impressed.

"Everything but the cake. I'm ordering that," she answers.

"Sarah has become an amazing cook," Loïc says proudly.

"Maybe you can teach me. I'm hopeless. My roommate, Kate, has tried to teach me, but it's just not in my nature." I shrug.

"If I can learn, anyone can." She turns back around and continues stirring.

"Do you want me to give Ev his bath and lay him down?" Loïc asks.

"Would you mind? I have a ton more to do in here."

"Of course. I'd love to."

I follow Loïc to the bathroom and watch as he bathes Evan. Loïc is so sweet with him, and it's obvious that this little boy adores him. The silly voices that Loïc uses to make Evan laugh are enough to set my ovaries on fire.

Like, seriously, impregnate me now.

Loïc dries Evan off with a fluffy bear towel, gets his diaper situated, and dresses him in his pajamas. I'm amazed at how easily he put that diaper on. I don't think I've ever changed a diaper in my life.

"You are so damn hot right now," I blurt out.

Loïc looks up from the rocker where he's holding Evan. "My Elmo voice turns you on?" He chuckles.

"All of it. It's weird, I know, but the last twenty minutes, it's the sexiest I've ever seen you."

"Okay," Loïc says, shaking his head with a wide grin.

"Maybe it's imagining you as a dad to our kids someday." The sentence comes out, and I don't regret it.

I realize that, tomorrow, Loïc and I will have only been back together for a week. But, after experiencing what it's like to be apart, I'm certain we'll never go through that again. This time is the real deal. I'm not in the mood to take it slow. I want Loïc, so it's full steam ahead. I want marriage and babies. I want the life. I want forever.

"So, how many kids do you want?" he asks me in a whisper as he continues to rock Evan.

"I'm not sure. I'd say at least two. I don't want an only child, but I'm not sure I could handle more than two either. Let's see how good of a mom I am to two, and then we can decide if any more would be a good idea."

"You'll be a great mom."

"I don't know if I will," I say truthfully.

"Well, I do."

"How are you so certain?"

"As a parent, all you need to do is love your child, and everything else works out. And, when you love, London, you love fiercely. I have no worries." He grins back at me. "So, I agree to two, and any more are to be determined."

"I like that—*to be determined*."

Loïc lays the baby down in his crib, and the two of us sneak out of the room and close the door.

"As long as I have you, the rest of my life can be *to be decided*. I'm open for anything, except for spending my life without you; that's nonnegotiable." Loïc pulls me against him and places a kiss on my forehead.

"I agree to those terms, sir."

"I'd like to continue this conversation in my room—naked. It'd also be hot if you threw in a few more *sirs* in there as well," he jokes before kissing and sucking on my neck.

I giggle as Loïc picks me up and carries me into his room.

It's hard to wrap my mind around this past week. For the first time in a very long time, I have no regrets, and my soul is completely at peace.

Loïc's right about one thing. I love him something fierce.

TWENTY

London

"There's nothing better than two whole and happy people being together, creating an epic love story."
—London Wright

Holding my cell to my ear, I continue my conversation with Paige, "Okay, listen, Paige. This is very important to me. Please?"

"You seriously want me to go to Loïc's after all this time to pick up a box of your old stuff? Can't you just buy them again?"

"No, these things are irreplaceable. I need them," I plead.

"And you're just now missing them?" She doesn't sound convinced.

"No, I've missed them the whole time, but I finally got Loïc to respond to an email about picking them up. He has them all boxed up and ready. You just have to go over there and get them for me."

"And he knows I'm coming?"

"Yes, he's expecting you, but it has to be right now, or he'll probably throw them away."

"That's rude," she says. "Okay, I'll head over there."

"Great. Look cute," I add.

"Why does it matter if I look cute?"

"Because I want my ex-boyfriend to see what he's missing by not dating me—my hot best friend." It's lame, but I'm not the best at coming up with lies in the spur of the moment.

"You're making no sense. Cali has made you weird."

"Okay, go now. Remember, it's urgent and imminent trash. Hurry," I say.

"What?" she asks, exasperated.

"You know, my stuff…in the trash…if you don't hurry. Go!"

I can hear her shuffling around on the other end.

"I'm on it. Call you in a few."

"Okay! Thanks, Paigey Poo!"

Fifteen minutes later, Paige is calling my cell.

"Hello?" I answer.

"He's having a big party. I can't go up to his house and ask for his ex-girlfriend's things while he's having a party."

"You have to, Paige. He said it had to be today, or he'd throw them out. Go. Go."

"Jeez, stop getting your shirt all in a twist. I'm going."

"It's panties. And thank you!"

A minute later, there's a knock on Loïc's door, and I pull it open wide. "Why, hello!"

Paige's mouth drops open. She looks around, like the porch is going to give her answers. "What's going on, London?"

"Oh…well, surprise! Loïc and I are back together!" I cheer as I pull Paige into a hug.

She's not quite to the stage of jumping up and down with her best friend because she's so happy, but I make her jump with me anyway.

Paige starts laughing. "What the hell, London? I'm so freaking confused!"

"Long story short, I ran into Loïc in LA. Turns out, he came for me last year, but he saw me with Brad. So, he left. He loves me, and I love him, so we're back together. He was in Cali with me this past week, and I came back here for a long weekend. I'll be here until Tuesday. Oh, and today is Sarah's baby's one-year birthday party. Yay!"

"Whoa, chica. You need to lay off the coffee." Paige chuckles and pulls me into another hug. "It's so good to see you." She squeezes me tight. "So, there's no box of stuff?"

"Nope. Just me." I grin. "I just thought it would be fun to surprise you."

"I'm definitely surprised." Paige looks around the foyer before whispering, "How are things with Sarah?"

"Pretty good. I don't think she's my biggest fan, but oh well. She and Loïc never hooked up, so I'm happy about that."

"No doubt. I have a feeling that you have so many more things to tell me."

"Oh, I do," I agree. "We'll have a girls' day tomorrow. Deal?"

"Deal."

"You have to see Loïc's nephew. He is the cutest thing ever. Come on." I pull Paige's hand and lead her toward the sliding glass door that opens to the backyard. "Oh, one more thing that I should warn you about, especially since Loïc is wearing shorts and the metal leg is pretty noticeable; Loïc lost his leg in Afghanistan. Feel free to ask him about it though. He's very open now. He's different…but the same, too."

Paige shakes her head. "Wow. This is crazy. And you are hopped up on some strong drug or something. You're way too happy."

"It's called the drug of love, Paige. The. Drug. Of. *Looove*." I grab her hand and pull her outside.

Paige laughs. "Tomorrow can't come fast enough. I need to find out what you've done to my best friend."

"I might have had one too many espressos," I admit with a giggle. "I didn't get much sleep last night, and this time difference is killing me."

"So, you're high on love and caffeine."

"Basically, yes," I nod exuberantly.

We reach Loïc where he's holding Evan. He's standing in a circle of people, including Sarah, Maggie, and Maggie's family. Cooper's sisters are here somewhere as well.

"Hey, Paige. Good to see you," Loïc says.

"Yeah, you, too," Paige answers.

"How was the surprise?" He chuckles, obviously noting Paige's still mildly confused expression.

"It was something. I was definitely surprised."

"I bet. Well, this is the birthday boy, Sarah's little guy. His name is Evan."

"Oh, he's so cute!" Paige exclaims as she reaches out to the baby to rub his chubby little hand.

"Told ya," I say.

I stand beside Maggie and give her a side hug as Paige continues to talk to Loïc and play with Evan.

"How's work, Mags?" I ask, happy to be around her again.

"It's good. Busy but good." She nods with a slight smile.

I think about how odd it still is for me to see Maggie without Cooper, and I have to ask, "How are *you*?" I know that she understands what I mean.

She forces out a small, sad chuckle. "I'm okay, London. Every day is still hard, but at the same time, each day gets a little easier. Does that make sense?"

I nod. "Yeah, it does."

"I'm thrilled for you and Loïc. I've always loved you two together. You're good for him. I love seeing him so happy," she says warmly, smiling toward Loïc.

"Thank you. I'm happy for us, too." I follow her gaze and find Loïc watching us with a big grin.

He winks at me, and I shake my head with a chuckle.

Out of the corner of my eye, I see Sarah as her head whips between Loïc and me, noticing our exchange. She leaves the group and walks back toward the house.

"I'm going to go see if Sarah needs any help in the kitchen," I say to the group.

"That's nice of you, babe." Loïc puckers his lips, and I meet them with mine, softly kissing him.

"I try." I shoot him a wink before heading inside.

When I get to the kitchen, Sarah is ladling coleslaw from a mixing bowl into a serving dish, but she's doing it with such force that little pieces of cabbage are flying out from the dish with each spoonful she throws in.

"Do you need any help?" I ask as cheerfully as possible.

Sarah's back stiffens, and she turns toward me. Her eyes are red with tears. "You? Help me? Oh, that's unlikely," she says with a huff, turning back to the bowl.

"Is something wrong, Sarah?" I attempt to extend an olive branch. I'm going to have to deal with this woman forever. It'd be nice if she didn't hate me.

She spins to face me again. "If you want to help me, you'll leave. Go back to LA, and stay away from Loïc."

"I can't do that," I say with a shake of my head.

"You ruin everything. I was so close. He just needed a little bit longer. Loïc is meant to be with me, London. Me! Not you. You can't possibly begin to understand him or what he's been through. I do." A tear falls down her cheek.

Although the majority of me thinks she's an extreme bitch, a part of me knows that she's just hurting. "I'm so sorry that you're upset, Sarah. I am. Truly. I know what it's like to love someone so much and not be able to be with him. But I'm not sorry for loving Loïc. He wants to be with me just as much as I want to be with him. I'm not going anywhere. I can guarantee that.

"We need to learn to get along. Maybe, someday, we could even be friends. You can't make Loïc choose between us because I can guarantee you that you wouldn't be happy with his choice.

"And you're right. No, I don't know his past as well as you do. But I don't need to understand everything he's been through. I just have to love him through it. You have his past, I know that, and I'm glad you had each other. But I have his future, and that's not going to change."

I turn, leaving Sarah with her mouth agape, and I head back out to the party.

"Everything all right?" Loïc asks when I reach him.

"Everything's great." I wrap my arms around him and hug him tight.

184

Paige is holding Evan up and spinning him around as he giggles incessantly.

I sure hope Sarah comes to her senses because I would hate for anything to happen that'd put stress on Loïc's relationship with his nephew.

Gosh, why do girls have to be such emotional basket cases?

I laugh to myself, thinking about how I was post-Loïc breakup. I was such a mess that I had to move across the country.

"What're you laughing about?" Loïc asks.

"You."

"What about me?"

"Just how addictive you are. Detoxing from you is a major downer."

"Well, I'm not going anywhere, so there will be no more detoxing for you." He kisses me.

"Promise?"

"Promise."

"This is the life. I've missed this," I say to Paige as I lean back in the comfortable leather chair that's massaging my back while my pedicurist is massaging my feet.

"Don't you and Kate get mani-pedis?" Paige asks.

"Rarely. Kate is teaching me how to live the frugal life. Believe it or not, we give each other mani-pedis. We have this little foot-massaging kit and everything."

"You make enough money to afford a manicure every now and then." Paige looks over to me.

"I know, but Kate doesn't make as much as I do. So, we tend to live to her budget. It's actually been kinda fun. It's like an adventure to see how far you can make your money stretch. You saw what we did with our apartment."

"Yeah, I was super impressed. That was awesome. I still can't believe you didn't pay a designer."

"Nope. It was all us." The thought brings me pride.

"So, now that you're on this independent kick, are you just never going to touch your trust fund again or what?" Paige asks.

"No, I will—eventually. But for something important. I'm thinking I'll use it to buy a nice home for my family to live in someday."

Paige nods. "That's a good idea."

"Yeah," I agree.

Paige flips through the color swatches. "I think I'm going to go with glittery pink. I'm in the mood for glitter." She brings her eyes up to meet mine. "How's Georgia? I haven't heard from her in a while."

"She's good. She's actually in Madagascar, working with some world-renowned lemur expert."

"Really?"

"Yeah." I grin. "She's trying to save this species of lemur that's almost extinct. She and this scientist are trying to get the remaining few to mate."

"So, she's like a lemur love expert?"

"She's trying to be."

"Gosh, what an overachiever," Paige jokes. "Here I am, making ads to sell coffee, and she's over there, saving an entire species."

"I hear ya. Last week, I wrote about a local surfing competition, the latest Botox remedies, an NFL player's cheating scandal, and the rising occurrence of gang-related drive-by shootings in LA. Not really saving the world."

"Well, we all can't save the world, or there would be no one left to do the other stuff. We each have our strengths."

"True."

"How are your parents?"

"Good. Dad's as busy as ever, and Mom's in Mexico, taking a three-week course to become an acroyoga instructor."

"No way! That's awesome."

"I know. It's so crazy."

"Well, she's happy, she's healthy, and I'm sure your dad loves that she's extra bendy." Paige presses her lips together in a smirk.

"Ew, Paige. No, don't go there."

She laughs.

It's silent for a moment before Paige says, "I still can't believe all of this. You and Loïc are back together. You're back in Michigan. We had a barbeque yesterday at Cooper, Maggie, and Loïc's house. Sarah and Loïc are living together, and you're cool about that. It's all so surreal." There's a hint of awe in her voice.

"I know. It's a lot to take in. I can hardly believe it myself. It's been a whirlwind of a week." I sport a giant smile, thinking about it.

"And you feel good about it? No more heartbreaks on the horizon?" Paige inquires hesitantly.

My body freezes, and I hold back a giggle as the pedicurist rubs a rough stone against the bottom of my foot. "Yeah, I feel great. It's the real deal this time," I answer Paige through clenched teeth.

She chuckles at my discomfort.

I let out a deep breath of relief when the woman stops assaulting my foot and moves on to the polish portion.

"Loïc tells me that he doesn't believe in fate and all that, but I do," I say to Paige. "It's confusing though because I don't know why Cooper was destined to die, you know? He shouldn't have died. And Loïc's parents and the way he was treated as a child—none of that was meant to be. No way. I can't believe that." I shake my head in disgust from just thinking about Loïc as a sweet child, abused and alone. "So, for some things, I can't justify that it was meant to be. Instead, it's like one of life's unexplainable things.

"Yet, when it comes to Loïc and me, I truly think that the past year was meant to happen. Loïc and I were always great together, but we weren't great on our own. He had issues. I had completely different issues. We're not perfect now, by any means, but we've each grown so much over the past year. We've worked on ourselves and become whole and happy apart, which will make our relationship together even stronger."

"I can see that," Paige says.

"In my heart, I've always known that Loïc is the one for me, and it took so long to wrap my mind around the fact that we weren't together. But, if the last week is any indication, we're going to be reaping the rewards from our time apart for the rest of our lives."

There's nothing better than two whole and happy people being together, creating an epic love story. It's one of life's greatest gifts. I'm so grateful that I learned the lessons I was meant to along the way so that I now have the capacity to embrace it all.

"I'm so happy for you, London," my best friend says in earnest, a warm smile on her face.

I reach my hand over to her chair and gently squeeze her hand, letting her know how much I love her.

"Well, I've got nothing left to teach you," she jokes. "As they say, *The grass isn't always greener on the other side.*"

"You know what else they say?" I ask with a grin. "*The grass is greener where you water it,* my friend."

"This is just getting too deep now." In a dramatic fashion, Paige throws her head back against the cushioned chair, causing me to laugh.

"Maybe it's time I start giving you advice. You can hand me your torch of wisdom, and I can help you. How's your love life going?"

"On a scale of one to ten, an eleven," Paige answers with a huff.

My eyes go wide. "Really? Why didn't you tell me? Who's the guy?"

Paige squints her eyes toward me. "There's no guy, London. Hence, the eleven."

I shake my head. "No, if there isn't a guy, then it would be zero."

"No, one is the best, and *ten* is the worst. So, eleven is like *whoa* bad," Paige says.

I laugh. "You have it completely backward. *Ten* is a better score than *one*. Ten is perfect."

"You're obviously confused," Paige scoffs with a wave of her hand.

"For someone so smart, sometimes, I wonder how you make it through the day." I chuckle.

"Hey, I resent that." Paige pouts.

"It was a compliment of sorts."

Paige shrugs. "Eh, all right. So, where do you want to go to dinner?"

"Have I told you today how much I love you?" I grin.

"No, but I know you do. Why wouldn't you? I'm the best thing to happen to you since sliced bread." She gives me a wink.

"Yes!" I raise my hands in the air in victory. "Folks, we have a winner!"

The two of us laugh hysterically as our pedicurists try to hide their smiles.

I want to always remember this time in my life. I know life is often a struggle. But it's the difficult stuff that makes the happy parts so sweet, like the cherry on top.

TWENTY-ONE

London

> *"I don't think everyone is fortunate enough
> to find magical love, but I'm thanking
> my lucky stars that we were."*
> —London Wright

I've just put the final coat of paint on the living room wall when Loïc walks in the door.

"How was it?" I ask excitedly.

Loïc pulls me in for a kiss.

"It was great. They have a really nice VA here. It's huge. I like the guys in the PTSD group."

"Oh, that's wonderful," I say, relieved.

I want so badly for Loïc to be happy out here in LA, and I know his involvement with the veterans at the VA is a big part of his happiness.

"I told you it'd be fine." He leans in, sweetly kissing me again.

"I know. I just want everything to be perfect."

"It will be because we're together."

So much has changed in the past month. Loïc moved out to LA to live with me. We moved out of Kate's apartment and got our own place. Though his house back in Michigan is still technically his, he pretty much gave it to Sarah and Evan. I know Loïc misses Evan like crazy, but he will fly back one weekend a month to see him. He promises me that it's a great arrangement, and I want to believe him because I want this to work.

"What's this for?" He touches the space between my eyebrows.

"What?"

"You're all scrunchy here. What are you worrying about?"

"I just want you to be happy," I admit out loud.

"I am, London. I promise."

"Okay." I nod.

"The room looks great," he says as he scans my handiwork.

"Yeah, it does, doesn't it?" I agree.

I never thought I'd see the day when I enjoyed physical labor. Yet the awesome feeling I get from completing a project is pretty amazing.

"We're going to go shopping with Kate next weekend. You'll be amazed at the incredible things she finds. She has a gift for it."

"Cool. How's everything going with her new roommate?"

"Really great. She really likes her."

Loïc is looking down at me, smiling.

"What?"

"I just love you," he says.

"I love you, too." I wrap my arms around his middle and hug him tight. "You know, if you're not happy here, we can move anywhere. I've built up a pretty great résumé. I'd be able to get a good job almost anywhere."

"London, will you stop? I'm so happy here. I'd be happy anywhere as long as I was with you. Okay? Remember, I can go anywhere, too. There are veterans all over this country. No matter where we went, I'd be able to find a VA nearby where I could help. If you eventually want to get a job somewhere else, then great. It's kind of cool that we can go anywhere we want."

"That is pretty awesome," I say against his chest.

"It is." He glances around the room at my paint job again. "You know, this whole independent, get-things-done side of you is incredibly sexy."

"Oh, yeah?" I gaze into his sea-blue eyes. "More so than my privileged, pay-someone-to-do-it-for-me side? Because that girl still exists."

"Oh, that side of you is really sexy, too."

"So, basically, no matter what I do, you'll find me sexy?"

"Yep." He nods his head. "I love every single part of you, London Wright."

My heart is happy. "Me, too. I love every part of you," I agree.

"You know, we've never made love on a paint tarp before." He quirks up an eyebrow.

"No, we haven't. Another first?"

"Oh, I think so." He places his hands on my cheeks and pulls me into a deep kiss.

I adore the way he kisses me with a controlled love that's on the precipice of abandon.

Our kiss transforms from slow and worshipful to quick and beseeching, taking us to the point where not being together is excruciating.

The connection I share with Loïc when we're together intimately is something I can't put into words. It's pure euphoria. It's everything and the only thing, all at once. It's how I know we're meant for one another. There could never be anything more right.

Our clothes are tossed haphazardly around the room. Loïc's fingers grasp mine as he holds my arms over my head. My back slides against the tarp-covered floor as Loïc moves inside me. His eyes never leave mine as we make love.

"You sure you're up to this?" I ask Loïc as we drop our surfboards in the sand near the water's edge.

"Oh, yeah. Don't worry; the leg's waterproof."

"I know. It's just that I don't want you to hurt yourself," I say, worried.

Loïc laughs. "I know what it's like to be hurt, London. This is nothing. The waves are tiny today. It's a great day for me to practice."

"How do you know you'll be able to do it with your new leg?"

"Surfing is ninety percent core-muscle strength. I'm good," he says with an air of cockiness. He grabs my hand and runs it across his six-pack, evidence of his daily workouts.

"Yes, you're hot. Stop bragging." I playfully roll my eyes.

"We could have another first."

"What's that?" I ask.

"Sex in the ocean." He presses his lips together, and man, how I want to lean in and kiss them.

"Heck no," I say. "We've done it in a lake. That's going to have to do. I'm not sure all the salt in the ocean would feel pleasant." I crinkle my face up in faux pain.

"Okay." He laughs. "Have you done this since your first time with me?"

"A couple of times with Georgia," I admit.

Loïc's face beams. "Really? That's awesome."

"What?" I huff in mock annoyance. "I like outdoorsy stuff," I say before throwing in the word, "sometimes."

"Says the girl who barely made it through a short kayaking trip on one of our first dates."

"Oh, I made it through just fine. Don't exaggerate." I stick out my tongue.

Loïc grabs me and tackles me to the sand as I scream in a fit of giggles. After a minute, the lighthearted mood ends. Loïc's arms hold me close to him, and he buries his face in my neck and breathes me in.

"Loïc?"

"Yeah?" he exhales against my skin.

"You okay?"

He raises his head and peers into my eyes. His eyes are so full of emotion. "Sometimes, I can't believe we're finally here. I've been so lost for so long. I never knew to dream of this happiness because I never knew such joy existed. You're better than a dream come true, London."

My eyes well up with tears. "I know exactly what you mean. Thank you for finding me, Loïc."

He shakes his head. "It was you who found me, babe."

"You're lucky I'm a persistent girl."

"That, I am."

"Are you ready for me to show you my surfing skills?" I ask.

"Are you going to be able to get up on the board?" he teases.

I scoff. "Am I going to be able to get up on the board?" I repeat his question. "Oh, please. Just watch me."

I jump up from the sand and grab my board. Blowing him a kiss, I run out into the water. Loïc follows right behind me.

Loïc's wrong though. It wasn't just me who found him. If anything, we found each other. I thought I was happy before, but just like Loïc, I never knew such joy existed. I don't think everyone is fortunate enough to find magical love, but I'm thanking my lucky stars that we were.

TWENTY-TWO

London

*"The seconds right before my greatest dream
comes true bring a moment of pause, so I can
take it all in and be thankful."*
—London Wright

I finally find a parking space a few blocks down from our apartment. It's a shitty end to a shitty day. Everyone at work seemed to take a dose of crazy before coming to work today. It was quite the madhouse. But, soon, all will be better because I'll get to see Loïc.

It's funny because, the first year of my job, it was normal for me to get home at nine o'clock every night. I loved being at work. Yet, now that I have Loïc waiting for me at home, I find that I'm tons more efficient, finishing my articles in record time, so I can be home by dinner every night.

Loïc always has a delicious meal prepared for me when I walk in the door. Thank goodness I'm dating someone who can cook. I've come to accept my limitations. Cooking will never be one of my strengths.

I reach the front door of our apartment and find a large wicker basket with a pink ribbon tied around it. It's completely empty. A laminated piece of stationery is attached to the handle.

> I SPY WITH MY LITTLE EYE A BEAUTIFUL GIRL
> WITH SOME FLAWS.

I pick up the basket and open the door. Inside, I find a path of candles; there must be hundreds of them. The path is covered with an assortment of flower petals. Atop the candlelit path of petals, every foot or so, there are...

Packages of gummies?

I pick up the first bag of gummy bears. Attached to the package with a pink ribbon is a square piece of laminated stationery.

> FLAW #1: YOU HATE BEING CORRECTED AND LOVE BEING RIGHT. I LOVE THIS BECAUSE IT SHOWS THAT YOU ARE STRONG AND SELF-CONFIDENT—TWO ASPECTS OF YOUR PERSONALITY THAT I FIND EXTREMELY SEXY.

I run my finger across the words with a smile on my face. I place the bag of candy in the basket and pick up the next bag, which happens to be a package of sweet-and-sour gummy worms.

> FLAW #2: YOU'RE NOT THE MOST OUTDOORSY TYPE OF GIRL. I LOVE THIS FLAW BECAUSE I GET TO EXPERIENCE SO MANY FIRSTS WITH YOU. YOU DIDN'T

THINK YOU LOVED TO BE OUTSIDE, BUT
I THINK YOU'VE BEEN FINDING THAT
YOU DO.

I put the bag in the basket. He's right. He's totally been turning me toward the dark side. I think I love it because Loïc does. Love does crazy things.

I grab the next package of Swedish Fish.

FLAW #3: YOU CAN BE WHINY. I LOVE
THIS FLAW, AND ONLY GOD KNOWS WHY.
I SHOULD HATE IT, BUT IT TURNS ME ON
AND MAKES ME WANT YOU MORE. YOU'RE
HOT, EVEN WHEN A SCREECHY SOUND
COMES FROM YOU. GO FIGURE.

I laugh, putting the candy in the basket, and I pick up the next one.

FLAW #4: YOU CAN BE JEALOUS, BUT I
LOVE THAT BECAUSE I KNOW YOU
LOVE ME.

I think of the way I handled myself with Sarah at the birthday party. I'd say I've come a long way with my jealousy.

FLAW #5: YOU LOVE TO SHOP. I DON'T
KNOW IF I'LL EVER LOVE THIS ONE, BUT
I'LL GO WITH YOU BECAUSE I LOVE YOU.

I giggle. I'm a total pain when I shop. I don't blame him. I put the gummy rings in the basket and pick up the next.

FLAW #6: YOU LOVE SNOOTY PARTIES. I LOVE THIS FLAW BECAUSE YOU LOOK AMAZING WHEN YOU'RE ALL DRESSED UP, AND LET'S NOT FORGET ABOUT THE CLOSET SEX.

What a great night that was. I smile at the memory and place the package in the basket.

FLAW #7: SOMETIMES, YOU HAVE NO TACT, AND YOU SAY EXACTLY WHAT'S ON YOUR MIND. I LOVE THIS BECAUSE YOU MAKE ME LAUGH.

The bags of candy continue.

FLAW #8: YOU WORRY WAY TOO MUCH ABOUT ME. I LOVE THAT YOU WORRY BECAUSE I KNOW THAT YOU CARE. NO ONE HAS EVER MADE ME FEEL MORE LOVED THAN YOU.

FLAW #9: YOU CAN BE NEEDY. YET I NEED YOU JUST AS MUCH, SO WE'RE ALL GOOD.

FLAW #10: YOU CAN'T COOK. I LOVE THAT YOU SUCK IN THE KITCHEN BECAUSE IT'S SOMETHING THAT I CAN DO FOR YOU.

FLAW #11: SOMETIMES, YOU ARE SCARED TO TRY NEW THINGS. MY FAVORITE PART OF OUR LIFE TOGETHER IS EXPERIENCING FIRSTS WITH YOU.

FLAW #12: YOU'RE TOO BEAUTIFUL. THE OTHER WOMEN OF THE WORLD CAN'T COMPETE. OKAY, YOU GOT ME; IT'S NOT A FLAW. I JUST WANTED YOU TO KNOW HOW STUNNING I THINK YOU ARE, BOTH INSIDE AND OUT.

FLAW #13: YOU CAN BE OVERLY EMOTIONAL. I LOVE THIS BECAUSE IT JUST MEANS THAT YOU'RE PASSIONATE. YOU HAVE CONVICTIONS, AND YOU SEE THEM THROUGH. YOU MAKE ME SO PROUD EVERY DAY.

FLAW #14: YOU GREW UP PRIVILEGED. THIS ISN'T REALLY A FLAW BECAUSE WE DON'T CHOOSE HOW WE GROW UP. BUT I WANTED TO POINT IT OUT BECAUSE, ALTHOUGH YOU WERE GIVEN EVERYTHING, YOU STILL BECAME A WOMAN WHO LOVES THE PEOPLE IN HER LIFE WITH SO MUCH FEROCITY. OUR CHILDHOODS WERE POLAR OPPOSITES, AND MAYBE THAT'S WHY WE'RE PERFECT FOR EACH OTHER. THEY SAY OPPOSITES ATTRACT, AND THANK GOD THEY DO.

FLAW #15: YOUR HEART IS ONLY CAPABLE OF LOVING ME. YOU'RE LUCKY I HAVE THE SAME FLAW. I CAN ONLY LOVE YOU.

I pick up the final bag of gummy candy that sits in front of our bedroom door.

THE WORD FLAW HAS A NEGATIVE CONNOTATION, BUT I DON'T SEE IT THAT WAY. IF WE DIDN'T HAVE FLAWS, WE'D ALL BE THE SAME. OUR IMPERFECTIONS ARE WHAT MAKE US WHO WE ARE. WITHOUT ANY FLAWS, YOUR BASKET WOULD BE EMPTY. THERE'D BE NOTHING FOR ME TO HOLD ON TO, TO LOVE. BUT, AS IT TURNS OUT, MY FLAWED HEART LOVES YOU MORE THAN YOU MIGHT EVER KNOW.

COME INTO THE BEDROOM. I HAVE A QUESTION TO ASK YOU.

My lip trembles as I read his last note. I know what's coming, and still, I've never been more nervous. The seconds right before my greatest dream comes true bring a moment of pause, so I can take it all in and be thankful. I pull in a few calming breaths as tears stream down my face.

And I open the door.

Loïc is standing in the middle of our bedroom. His beautiful face is lit by the glow of candlelight. I take a few steps until I'm right across from him. I set the basket down next to me as Loïc drops to one knee and holds up a stunning diamond ring.

I bring my hands to my mouth with a gasp.

"London, you are the most important person in my life. You know that I've been dealt a tough hand in the past, but being with you creates such happiness, a bright light that lights up the darkness until I can't feel anything but love. You save me every single day. My flawed heart is capable of loving only you. I would love to spend this lifetime creating firsts with you, if you'll have me. London

Wright, will you do me the honor of becoming my wife? Will you marry me?"

"Yes! Yes! Yes! Yes!" I scream as I tackle Loïc to the ground before ravishing his mouth with mine. I jerk my lips away from his to say, "I love you so much, Loïc Berkeley. I'm going to love you forever."

Our mouths move as one until Loïc pulls away. "Can I put on the ring?" He chuckles.

"Yes! Of course." I climb off of him and hold out my hand.

My heart seems to freeze before I feel it pound forcefully in my chest. Holding my breath, I lean in as he places the ring on my finger. Tears continue to fall, and I smile wide. "It's the most beautiful ring I've ever seen."

Loïc's lips part as he breathes in. "Nothing but the best for my girl."

"You know I would have married you if you'd proposed with a Froot Loop, right?" I nudge my knee against his.

"But you're secretly thrilled with how pretty the ring is." His eyes shine with amusement.

"You know me so well." I throw my arms around him, pressing my lips against his once more.

Loïc's lips send me spiraling into a haze of lust and desire.

"Loïc, will you make love to your fiancée right here on the floor, surrounded by candles and flower petals?"

A slow, sexy smile forms on his lips as he threads his fingers through my hair. His expression now lusty and primal, he says, "Yes, yes, and yes."

Loïc crashes his mouth against mine. My body instantly responds to him. Our tongues move desperately against each other. I just can't get enough of him. I want him with an unyielding urgency.

"How do you want it, babe?" Loïc asks even though I know he already knows. He knows me better than anyone.

"I want it hard, so hard," I pant.

In one swift movement, Loïc has me on the ground. With my back pressed against rose petals, he stretches my legs, pushing them against my chest.

He enters me in one quick thrust that I can feel all the way in my belly. I cry out in pleasure. The room fills with the sound of skin slapping against skin as Loïc plunges into me, filling me up with immense satisfaction.

When Loïc takes me this way, hard and fast, it's incredible. The buildup is quick, and the release is sudden and intense.

I grab at Loïc's slick chest, my hands sliding across his hard muscles. I can't think straight as I moan eagerly.

Finally, I just close my eyes and allow the mind-blowing sensations to pull me under. My nerves are on fire, and each time Loïc enters me, a wave of heat sends ripples of ecstasy through my body to the very tips of my fingers and toes.

My release builds, a bold crescendo within me begging to reach its peak. I cry out Loïc's name over and over as he takes me higher. Rocking back and forth, he thrusts, and the pleasure is enough to curl my toes.

Shock waves pulse through me as I fall over the edge, my entire body quivering. Loïc growls as his body shudders when he releases inside me.

He falls atop me, and I wrap my limp arms around his back as we work to calm our breaths.

"That was amazing," I say on a sigh.

He kisses my shoulder. "It was a very good start." His voice drops an octave, making him sound all husky and sexy.

"A start?" I giggle.

"Babe, there's nowhere else I want to be but inside you tonight. I want to make love to you until we can't see straight."

"That sounds like a fantastic plan." With my fingertips, I lightly trace circles across his back.

"Doesn't it?" he asks, a smile present in his voice.

His fingers trail up my sides, leaving goose bumps in their wake. He kisses up my neck until his mouth is on mine once more.

As I move my tongue against his, images of wishes for my future flicker through my mind. In each one, I'm with Loïc, and in each one, I'm happy.

TWENTY-THREE

Loïc

> *"I didn't have to fly across an ocean to find peace because London found me."*
> —Loïc Berkeley

Blinking rapidly, I struggle to focus on the number on the door. "Well, it's thirty, right?" I ask London, biting my lip.

"Yep, flat thirty. This is it." London grabs ahold of my hand and runs her free hand up and down my arm. "Are you okay?"

"Yeah," I lie.

"Look at me."

I close my eyes and turn to face London. I release an audible breath before opening my eyes to find London's brown-eyed gaze roaming over me, enveloping me. A slow smile forms on her lips, lighting up her eyes, and this simple gesture sheds light into the dark corners of my mind, extinguishing my inferno of nerves.

Freeing my hand, she wraps her arms around my neck. My mind is full of dueling emotions, both fear and love. Yet, as always, London's love wins. When our lips meet, a sense of calm permeates, crowding out my panic.

"Better?" she asks breathlessly as she pulls her lips from mine.

"Yeah," I say.

"Whatever happens, you'll be fine. Right?"

I nod in agreement.

Uncertainty reappears as I reach out and knock on the door, but London's right. I can deal with whatever I find.

The door remains closed, so I knock again.

A woman who appears to be in her thirties opens the door. She looks quite exhausted with a toddler on her hip, who is covered in some sort of red sauce. "Yes? Can I help you?"

I clear my throat. "Hi, I'm looking for my grandparents. They used to live here. Henry and Jane Berkeley?"

The woman thinks for a moment. "No, I haven't heard those names. I've been here for about five years, and before that, it was a guy named Jay and his husband. I'm sorry. I wish I could help you."

"That's okay. Thank you," I say.

She nods and closes the door.

I turn to London. "Well, shit, that was anticlimactic."

She laughs. "Yep, kinda was."

"I suppose we should drive down and see if they still own the cottage," I suggest.

"Sounds like a plan," London agrees as we head outside to our rental car.

"Look," I say to London before we get in the car. "You can see Big Ben from here."

It took me a long time to make it here. It's surreal that I'm finally in London, the place I held on to as a child through all the darkness. It was my dream, my happy place. I thought, when I made it here, I would be safe. I would find joy.

I breathe in, taking in my surroundings. The landmarks that I've seen in photos my whole life—structures that equated to my promised land, my sanctuary—are all around me. Yet, as I turn to *my* London—my living, breathing beautiful girl—joy expands in my chest, and warmth fills my body, bringing a smile to my face.

I didn't have to fly across an ocean to find peace because London had found me. She's the answer to every question. She's the solution to every problem. With her love, I can do anything.

She catches me watching her. "What?" she says with a smile, making my heart twist a little.

"Just you."

"Just me?"

"I just need you." I hold her gaze with mine.

The sides of her lips quirk up into a smile. "And I just need you."

"Ready?" I ask.

"Ready," London answers.

We open the car doors and get in.

We set the GPS to take us out of London, southwest, toward the Lulworth area of Dorset, where my grandparents' cottage is—or at least used to be.

I'm focusing on driving on the opposite side of the road. "It's weird, driving over here."

"It is." London chuckles, looking up from her phone. "Every time I look out the window, I have a momentary freak-out, thinking we're on the wrong side." She returns her attention to her phone. "So, I'm reading about this Lulworth area, and it sounds pretty cool. There's this gorgeous cove, and according to this map, I think that's where your grandparents' cottage is. There's also this big stone archway that extends into the water; it's called the Durdle Door. It looks awesome." She chuckles. "Durdle Door," she says again quickly. "That sounds like Dumbledore."

"What's Dumbledore?" I ask with a quirked eyebrow.

"Wow, we've got to catch you up, my love."

Out of the corner of my eye, I can see London shaking her head.

"Dumbledore is only the greatest wizard of all time."

"What are you talking about?" I laugh.

"You know, Harry Potter, Dumbledore," she responds with a hint of mirth in her voice.

"I've never watched Harry Potter," I reply.

"Well, when I lived with Kate, I started sharing all my favorite TV shows with her, so she made me read all of her favorite books. I mean, it's not like she *made* me. I wanted to. So, I read the seven Harry Potter books, and then one weekend, we did a marathon of the eight movies. It was so awesome. You have to read those books," London says in awe.

"Eight movies?"

"They made the last book into two movies."

I nod. "I see."

"Oh, they have a castle in the Lulworth area, too!" London exclaims excitedly.

"You know, I think I remember my dad telling me a story about that castle. He always made England seem so magical."

"It kind of is, if you think about it. So much history. I wish we had castles."

"Our country's just a baby compared to the countries in Europe," I say as I accidentally drive around a roundabout twice, not able to figure out which road to get off on.

London laughs. "That one." She points toward the correct exit.

"I knew that." I give her a wink.

"I don't know why we didn't think of it when we were at your grandparents' old flat, but we should have knocked on the neighbors' doors. Some of their neighbors might have remembered them."

"Yeah, you're right. Well, depending on what we find here, we can always go back and do that."

In three hours' time, we're driving down the coast of Lulworth, and then I'm pulling into the drive of the cottage.

"Oh my gosh, this is it?" London asks, pressing her hand against her chest, her fingers splayed out.

I lean in toward the windshield to get a better view as I turn off the car. "This is it."

"It's like a fairy-tale cottage. It's amazing." London is still as she looks around the property.

I nod, hardly able to believe we're here.

It's a classic English cottage with stone siding, a tiled roof, and green vines and foliage growing up the walls. The property is surrounded by a stone fence, also adorned in greenery.

"After all this time, it looks exactly the same. We had a picture in our house of my dad standing in front of this place when he was younger. Someone lives here. It's well taken care of," I tell London.

We exit the car and walk up to the white wooden door. I knock.

I knock again.

"No one's here," I say on a sigh, stating the obvious.

"Well, that sucks," London says, also stating the obvious.

I scan the house, not sure of what I'm looking for. *I just came all this way…*

A birdhouse hanging from a metal hook with a ceramic red bird atop it catches my attention. Squinting, I study it. For some reason, it seems similar.

"I think I remember…" I say as I grab the bird and pull up.

Sure enough, it lifts off the house, and beneath it is a key.

"How'd you know that was there?" London asks.

"I'm not sure exactly. I recall bits and pieces of a story my dad told me. I can't remember the details exactly. But something told me to pick up that bird."

"So, should we go in?" London looks at me, and a slow smile forms on her lips, lighting up her eyes.

I shrug with a laugh. "Might as well."

"I mean, we have the key. It's not breaking and entering if you have a key."

I put the key in the lock and turn. "Exactly."

Once inside, there's no question that my grandparents still own the cottage. The evidence is staring back at me through every framed photograph that decorates the walls and surfaces.

"Is this you?" London grabs a frame from an end table with a picture of a five-year-old version of myself smiling.

"Yeah, it is." I take the photo from her and stare at the little boy smiling back.

He's showing the person behind the camera a Star Wars Lego ship that he built. He's so proud and happy. I remember getting that ship for Christmas.

An ache for the little boy resonates from deep within my chest. If he only knew what two years' time would bring...

I mourn his smile, the one he's so freely giving now, the one that will soon all but disappear because he won't have anything worth smiling about. I want to reach inside the frame and warn him of everything to come, to urge him to lock every happy moment of the next two years in his mind so that he'll have those memories later.

But I can't because I've already lived it.

"You were so cute." London wraps her arm around my back, leans her head against my arm, and stares at the photo in my hands. "So happy and so loved."

I was loved, I think to myself as I look at the photo again.

I place the framed photo back where it was.

"I know you were adopted, but it's crazy how much you look like him," London says as she stares at a picture of my parents hanging on the wall.

"I remember Nan telling me that I was meant to be adopted by my parents because I resembled my dad when he was little, and God knew that she wanted another blue-eyed boy to squeeze."

"Well, you definitely resemble him. It's surreal." She hands me the photo.

My parents are facing each other. Mom's arms are wrapped around Dad's neck. They look like they're dancing. My mom's head is thrown back in laughter. My dad's eyes gleam with mirth as he faces the camera. It's odd, seeing my mom so happy. In all my memories, she was sad, heartbroken for the babies her body couldn't carry. I want to remember her like this—young and joyously in love.

London and I make our way around the room, taking in each picture, speculating about the event that went along with the happy moment in my family's life. Each photo represents a time that was special enough that my grandparents wanted to remember it—to capture it, frame it, and give it a presence within their home.

It's hard to put into words what it feels like to actually see my parents' faces again. All these years, I've tried so hard to remember the details of their faces. But time dulls memories, and as each year went by, the details blurred into each other until they were mere shadows in my mind.

"Do you remember this one?" London asks, handing me a photo containing everything that was good with my childhood.

I'm sitting on my dad's lap. My mom is next to us on the couch. Her arm is around my father as she leans her head against his shoulder. My grandparents are wrapping their arms around us all, leaning in from behind the couch. All five of us are wearing giant smiles full of genuine joy and love.

Closing my eyes, I breathe out of my nose, long and heavy. Dueling emotions battle within me. Seeing all their faces causes a surge of grief to consume me, but at the same time, I can't stop the smile that comes to my face as the memory returns.

I open my eyes to look at London. "Yeah, I remember it. This was the last Christmas that we were all together. My dad had set up the automatic timer on the camera. He had it stacked on top of many books and boxes to get it at the right level for the photo. My granddad was obsessed with wasps, and he knocked over the tower of stuff holding the camera in an attempt to kill them." Elation expands in my chest at the memory. "I remember my dad running to the camera to make sure it wasn't broken, and Nan almost fell over a chair while trying to get to Granddad before he broke anything else."

"Wasps?" London smiles in question.

I shake my head. "I can't remember what that was all about. I don't remember any bugs in the house. I just recall laughing at my granddad and his silly antics. I don't think Nan thought Granddad was as funny as I did though. It's crazy…" I stare at the photo again. "You would never know by looking at this picture that the moments leading up to it were filled with so much chaos. We just look like the perfect happy family."

"You were," London states, the corners of her mouth tilting up into a smile. "Life isn't the posed smiles for a camera. It's the beautiful chaos that surrounds the picture. Your life was perfect because you were enveloped in love."

I stare down to London. Her eyes capture mine, and a surge of gratitude for this woman encircles me.

My pulse leaps when an angered voice cuts across the room. "What are you doing in here?"

London and I jump back from each other with startled gasps. An older woman is standing in the doorway with her cane raised, ready to strike.

"I'm sorry. I was just—" I start to explain.

The woman's mouth falls open. "Blimey, it's you," she says in wonder. She returns her cane back down to the floor. "You're the grandson."

"Hi, I'm Loïc Berkeley." I extend my hand, and the woman shakes it.

"I'm Esther Willis, the caretaker of this place."

"You're the caretaker?" I ask, returning the photo of my family to the shelf where London found it.

"Yes, though my grandson does most of the work at this point. It's been a long time." She stares up at me, and I feel as if the last sentence was a reprimand of sorts.

"Do you know where my grandparents are?"

She nods. "Follow me."

She leads us to one of the bedrooms. Using her cane, she smacks the side of a box that's sitting on the bed. "In there, you'll find everything you need—letters, legal documents, a deed to this house, their will."

"So, they've passed," I say out loud for myself more than anything.

"Jane, yes. It's...let's see...coming up on twenty years now, I believe. Right before your parents' accident, she was diagnosed with an aggressive form of breast cancer. She was actually in surgery when your parents passed. I've never seen her so distraught as when she heard the news." Esther stares off to the ground. "Jane was my best friend. We were pregnant with our sons at the same time." She smiles to herself.

"Anyway," Esther continues, "she was so sick, you see. She wasn't cleared for travel. She talked to the government people over there, and they said they would place you with a nice family until she could make arrangements to get you. But...she never got better." Esther looks past me, as if she's remembering. Releasing an audible sigh, she says, "She wrote to you every day. The letters were all returned. They're in the box." She nods toward the bed.

"What about my grandfather?"

"He's still alive."

When I hear those words, I draw in a deep breath, my pulse leaping. "A couple of years prior to Jane's death, he was diagnosed with early-onset Alzheimer's. He couldn't come get you because he could barely take care of himself. He was put into a home shortly before Jane's passing. He's still there. Unfortunately, his mind is gone. I've been up to see him a few times, but he doesn't know who I am, let alone who he is. Alzheimer's is a miserable way to go…steals your mind but leaves your body. Just terrible." She shakes her head.

"I'm sorry," she says. "But he did have many years with periods where he was still himself, and he wrote to you a lot." She eyes the box once more.

The room is exploding with an uncomfortable silence, save for the breaths of its occupants. I pull in air as I try to process everything I just heard.

Esther clears her throat. "I'm so sorry," she repeats.

"It's okay," I reassure her.

"I promised Jane I would look for you to let you know about her and Henry. I tried, but I didn't know how. You wouldn't believe how difficult it is to navigate through another country's social services. Remember, this was before the Internet is the way it is now. There were phone calls and letters, neither of which proved to be of any use in finding you. I just hoped that you were raised by a nice family and that, someday, you'd come here for answers. And here you are." She smiles warmly.

"Well, this cottage is yours. There's account information in the box. All the bank accounts are in your name. There's a pretty large life insurance policy that you can collect as well. I don't know what your plans are, but my grandson will gladly keep this place up, if needed. I'll write down my contact information for you and leave it on the table by the door in case you have any questions. I'll just give you some time." She nods and turns toward the door.

"Excuse me, Ms. Willis?" I ask before she leaves.

"Yes, dear?"

"Where is my grandfather exactly?"

"Oh." She walks back in the room and pulls a pamphlet from inside the box. "He's here." She hands it to me and exits the room.

On the floor of the bedroom, London and I sit cross-legged amid a bunch of papers. There are official documents and personal letters from Nan, Granddad, and Ms. Willis.

"Look at this one." I show London. "It was addressed to me when I was in New Hope, living with Dwight and Stacey. Do you think they are the ones who marked it with *Return to sender*? Why would they have done that?"

The hurt little boy that so desperately wanted to know he was loved mourns within my soul.

"I don't know." London looks down at the letter in my hand. "There are such cruel people in this world."

We continue reading letter after letter. I hear London sniffle, and I look over to find her wiping her eyes.

"They loved you so much, and all this time, you thought they didn't." Her voice breaks as she shakes her head. "It just breaks my heart. I can feel your Nan's pain through her words. None of this is fair," she says with a half-sob.

My heart thrums wildly. "No, it's not."

The evening is spent soaking in the memories my grandparents left me, and they left me a lot. Nan's letters are full of stories about her and my grandfather when they were younger, my father growing up, and the tales of how my parents met, how they found me, and how they loved me.

In the few months she was able to fight her sickness, she documented a lifetime of memories. It's the greatest gift she could have left me. For someone who has lived a life full of unanswered questions, finally gaining the facts of one's heritage is an overwhelming and powerful experience.

I now have stories of a family that loved me and loved each other. I have a past and history that extends beyond torture and heartbreak. I plan to read these letters over and over again—not tonight, but soon. I want to cement my Nan's beautiful words into my mind, turning them into memories, allowing them to shed light on all the dark corners of my mind.

London and I sit out on the back patio and listen to the waves from the sea as we eat a dinner of granola bars and water, which was what we had in the car. Neither of us has any interest in leaving the cottage tonight.

Years of love are penetrated into the walls, the furniture, the air; it's almost tangible as it surrounds me. Maybe it's finally having answers, perhaps it's the letters or this cottage, or it's a combination of all three, but I've discovered a sense of myself that I never knew was there.

TWENTY-FOUR

Loïc

"It's not England that's magical; it's life."
—*Loïc Berkeley*

"You know what amazes me?" London asks on our drive to the nursing home that houses my granddad. Her question is rhetorical because she continues, "The cottage felt lived in even though no one had stayed there for years. I mean, the sheets smelled like they had been freshly washed. Nothing had dust on it. The air didn't have the stale smell that abandoned places get."

"Yeah."

"I think Ms. Willis has been cleaning that cottage, waiting for you to come, for almost twenty years. That's commitment." She reaches over and places her hand on my thigh.

"You're right. She could have been keeping it nice in memory of Nan, too. They were best friends," I offer.

"It's probably a little bit of both," London agrees. "Are you feeling okay about today?"

"I'm sure it's going to be strange, seeing him, especially since he won't know me. But a selfish part of me is glad that I have a living family member even if just physically. Is that horrible?"

She shakes her head. "No, of course not. I understand. He's still your granddad, and he's alive. That's exciting."

The nursing home is two hours north of the cottage even though it seems further. I'm relieved when we finally arrive.

We check in at the front desk, and a few minutes later, someone comes to get us.

"Hello, I'm Nancy, one of the nurses who works with Mr. Berkeley."

I like Nancy immediately. With her bright eyes and warm smile, I can tell that she's one of those people who's everyone's friend. It makes me feel good, knowing that Granddad gets to see her happy face every day.

"So, you're the grandson?"

"Yes. I live in the United States." I explain to Nancy a little about my past and how I just found out yesterday that my granddad was alive.

London and I follow Nancy as she walks down a hallway. "Well, I'm glad you came. Mr. Berkeley hasn't had a visitor in years. Have you been around someone with Alzheimer's before?"

"No, I haven't."

"Well, the main thing to understand is that he won't know you, so don't take it personally. That's just the way it is with Alzheimer's patients. Most days, Mr. Berkeley doesn't speak at all. Every now and again, he's lucid enough to talk, but what he says doesn't normally make any sense to the rest of us. You can talk to him, of course. We're not sure how much our patients can understand—the reality is, probably not much—but it doesn't hurt to try."

"How long can someone live with Alzheimer's?" I ask.

"The average is ten years past diagnosis. However, it varies. Truthfully, your grandfather has survived more years than most. It's difficult. His mind has gone, but his body refuses to. He doesn't appear to be in any physical pain or mental anguish, which is the best we can hope for." She smiles. "There he is." She points to a man sitting in a chair by the window in what appears to be a large living room area. "Let me know if you need anything. I'll be around."

I look to London. She entwines her fingers through mine, and we walk toward my granddad. Releasing her hand, I pull up two chairs and set them in front of him.

He looks the same, like the man from the pictures I vaguely remember, but older and paler. His hair is now completely gray, and his face wears more wrinkles. I feel a weak yet familiar pull toward him. I'm not sure what I expected, but I hoped for a strong, real connection. I want my heart to know he's family and to feel something, anything.

He doesn't acknowledge us sitting in front of him.

"Just talk. Tell him about yourself," London urges in a whisper.

"Hi, Granddad. It's me, Loïc, your grandson."

I look to my granddad and wait. He doesn't move his stare from the window.

I turn my head to face London.

"I know," she says gently. "But we don't know what he understands, so just keep talking. Tell him stories about your life."

"Okay." I nod.

I've craved a familial connection for so long, but the man before me isn't the same as the one I remember. He isn't laughing, making jokes, or driving Nan crazy. He's not doing anything, and it's unsettling.

Yet I do as London suggested. I talk.

I pretend that my granddad is listening and able to care. He's not the same man I hoped to see, but maybe deep down, part of that man still lives.

There's a chance he hears me. So, I tell him about being in the military. I talk about meeting Sarah while in foster care and how she's become like a sister to me. I smile big when I mention Evan. I glance at London with nothing but affection in my eyes as I tell this man all about the woman I love and how we're going to get married.

Through it all, he never looks at me or shows signs of knowing that I'm there. This interaction leaves me with a slight sadness in my heart.

"I don't know what else to say," I tell London.

"Oh, I know! I'll tell him how you proposed."

London turns to my granddad and goes on and on with so much excitement, telling him every detail of the proposal. Well, at least up to the point when she said yes. He doesn't need to know what happened after that.

I watch, fascinated, as she speaks to this man, as if he's interested, as if he's talking back with her. She doesn't end with the proposal. She continues with stories of our time together. She tells him about my work with veterans and the speech I gave when she saw me again for the first time.

It's bizarre because, as I listen to London and this one-sided conversation, it's as if she's sitting here, having a legitimate conversation with my grandfather. She pauses and laughs and tells the stories with enthusiasm and love. In this moment, I fall in love with her a little more.

After a couple of hours, we decide to go.

I touch my granddad's arm and say, "We'll come back another day, okay?"

As I pull my hand away from his arm and stand, he turns his head and looks at me. I freeze and stare into his eyes.

He blinks. His voice is hoarse as he says, "William?"

He thinks I'm my dad.

"Yeah." I nod.

"How are you, son?" He reaches his arm out and takes my hand.

"I'm good, Dad," I answer.

"Where's little Loïc? Did you bring him?" he asks, hopeful.

I shake my head. "Not today."

"You must bring him to visit. Your mom and I just adore that boy. He's a special one, isn't he? Such a gift." A small smile touches his face before his eyebrows crinkle. "Where's your mom?" he asks, almost panicked.

"She's coming. She's on her way."

"Good, good. I miss her."

"She misses you," I say.

His grip on my hand releases, and he drops his hand to his lap. He closes his eyes and then opens them again. When he does, he's gone. The blank expression has returned.

"Dad? Granddad?"

There's no sign that he hears me as he looks out the window again.

225

I turn to London to find her eyes red with tears.

"That was amazing," she says, reaching out to grab my hand.

I take hers in mine and squeeze softly.

"Yeah." I shake my head in awe at what just happened.

"Try again," London urges.

"Okay."

I gently grip my granddad's arm and say, "We're going to get going now, Granddad. We'll be back another day, okay?"

I wait for a response, but there's nothing, and it's all right.

As we walk out of the home, the reality that something like that might never happen again sets in. Yet I'm oddly fine with it because I feel like I was just given a gift. My granddad came back to life, if even for a few seconds, and it was magical. He didn't know who I was, but he loved me. They all did. None of them wanted to leave me, but they weren't given the choice.

Nan was right. It's not England that's magical; it's life. Sometimes, one can pray for a miracle, and it never comes. And, other times, one might not know they need one, yet they get a miracle anyway.

Now, almost twenty years later, I finally know the truth.

The one and only truth is love. I've had it all along, and I finally believe in it.

TWENTY-FIVE

London

*"True joy comes when one's heart is
completely open and vulnerable to the world."*
—London Wright

The sun is just starting to warm the earth with its light. Its
rays sneak into the bedroom between the fluttery white
curtains that dance from the salty air of the sea.

After visiting Loïc's granddad yesterday, we came
back to the cottage where we plan to stay for the rest of
our vacation.

I can't remember a time in my life when I've been so
happy. The obvious reason for that is because there
hasn't been one.

It's hard to wrap my mind around the past three
years.

I think of that girl who basically rubbed her boobs
against Loïc's dirty truck that hot May day. In hopes of
what? A booty call, a one-night stand, attention? *Who was*

she? God, I barely recognize her. *How did she ever win over Loïc?*

I was never a bad person. I did the best I could with the knowledge I had of the world, and at that point, I was looking through entitled, spoiled, rose-colored glasses.

Loïc thinks I saved him, but he's wrong. He saved me. He saved me from myself, from me living a shallow, self-centered existence. I know that sort of life would never have led to happiness. No one can live a life of genuine happiness without experiencing the gift of loving someone more than themselves. True joy comes when one's heart is completely open and vulnerable to the world. Yes, with that vulnerability comes potential for great pain, but the pain is what allows us to appreciate the love. Loïc taught me that. Change comes with knowledge. As soon as I knew better, I demanded more from my life.

"What were you giggling about?" Loïc's tired but alluring voice whispers from behind me as his arm that's wrapped around my middle pulls me against him.

His firm chest against my back causes an intoxicating pressure to start to build within me. I turn around to face him, immediately lost in his impossibly blue depths.

"What was funny?" he asks again with a sly grin.

He knows I can't think straight when confronted with a Loïc who's just woken up. His hair all tousled and his sleepy expression just make me want him more.

I blink, clearing my lust-hazed mind. "Oh, I was just thinking how much things have changed since the car wash."

"God, have they ever." He lets out a chuckle, raspy and sexy, from deep within his chest.

I place my lips against his skin, and his pectoral muscles tighten at the contact.

"I love it here," I whisper between kisses.

"Me, too."

"We need to come here a lot." I kiss my way down his stomach.

"We will," he says with a pant.

My hand that's splayed across his chest can feel the wild beating of his heart as my other hand explores beneath his boxers before pulling them off.

I take Loïc in my mouth, and he groans in pleasure, his fingers pulling at the bedsheets. There is nothing I love more than rendering Loïc completely helpless with want. I crave his release. Watching him come undone with ecstasy is one of my favorite things.

When he's finished, I kiss up his body. With every touch of my lips, I'm saying a prayer of gratitude. *Thank you for this man. Thank you for this life. Thank you.*

"I love you," he utters breathlessly when I reach his face.

The adoration that radiates off of him in waves is so tangible that I can feel it hit my skin, absorb, and then permeate my soul with a satisfaction so fulfilling that it aches.

"I love you," I say back. Those three little words don't seem to be enough, as they could never carry the entire weight of what I feel. Ever.

In one swift move, Loïc flips us so that my back is against the sheets. In a matter of seconds, we're one as he enters me hard and fast. There are occasions for slow, sweet, and savory—gentle kisses, words of devotion, and heated breaths. Then, there are times when the need is so great that nothing quenches it but quick and forceful— bed-shaking, toe-curling, animalistic moaning, and skin-slapping with all-consuming love. And Loïc always knows how I need it.

ELLIE WADE

"Who said England wasn't magical?" Loïc states through panted breaths as we lie beside each other in post-orgasmic euphoria.

"Supernatural, exquisite, freaking fantastic," I stammer out.

"Well, now you're just giving me a big head."

"Oh, you're right. I wouldn't want that. Gotta keep you reaching for perfection."

"Exactly."

I roll toward the center of the bed, placing my face against Loïc's chest. "Do you remember our first Twenty Questions game?" A surge of gratefulness and nostalgia passes through me.

"You mean, on the plane?"

"Yeah."

Loïc laughs softly. "Of course. You were a persistent and nosy little thing."

My lips turn up into a giant smile. "You were acting all broody, angry, and closed off."

"I was all those things." His fingers lightly trace circles across my back. "But you wouldn't back off, no matter what. My little tenacious firecracker."

"Hey, I know what I want," I say without apology.

"That quality is one of my favorite things about you. I love your spirit," Loïc says. Although I can't see his face, I know he's smiling. "I loved opening my email to see your questions every day during deployment."

He sighs, and I know his mind is now elsewhere.

"Ask me a question," I say cheerfully, looking up toward Loïc's face.

He kisses me on the tip of my nose. "I think we know all there is to know about each other, don't you?"

"No way. I'll never be ready to stop discovering new things about you."

230

"All right. Well, you go first. I have to think of a question."

"Okay. If you could live anywhere in the world, where would you live?"

"That's easy," he answers. "Wherever you are."

"No, that's cheating. If I weren't in the picture and money and jobs weren't factors, where would you live?"

"It's not cheating if it's the truth," he says with a grin.

"Just answer." I playfully poke him in the side.

"Fine. If it were just me and nothing else was a factor…" He pauses. "I honestly can't think of a specific place. I think the main thing is that I would want to live somewhere beautiful, somewhere where I'd prefer to spend my time outdoors instead of inside. I think endless locations could qualify. Maybe here?"

"It is gorgeous here. We should go explore today," I suggest.

"Yeah, that sounds awesome," Loïc agrees.

"Did I mention that I love it here?"

"Yeah, once or twice." His deep chuckle makes something within my heart twist.

Loïc's cell rings from the bedside table. Extending his free hand, he grabs it. "Hello?"

I give him space as he sits up.

"Yes, this is he."

I sit up as well, pulling the sheet around me, as I listen to his side of the conversation.

"Really? How? Yeah, right. I understand. Okay. Yeah. Yeah. I will. Thank you." Loïc ends the phone call, dropping the cell phone to the bed. He sits motionless, staring at the opposite wall, before he turns to me. "My granddad passed away last night."

Gasping, I cover my mouth with my hands. My eyes fill with tears as I shake my head. "No." I cover Loïc's hand with mine. "How? What happened?"

"That was the nurse, Nancy. She said he died peacefully in his sleep last night. She said there was nothing wrong with him physically; it was simply just his time. I have to figure out what I want them to do with his body and call her back."

"I'm so sorry, Loïc."

"It's okay. I'm glad we got to see him." His voice drifts off.

"We don't even know where your Nan is. We should call Esther and ask. Your granddad should be laid to rest with her. They would want that."

Loïc nods. "Yeah, they would."

Several minutes of silence pass.

Loss is a delicate thing. It's hard to know what someone needs, but I think the most important thing is that Loïc knows I'm here for him. So, I wait as Loïc thinks, and I continue rubbing his hand.

"London?" he asks after a bit.

"Yes?"

"I know it sounds silly, but do you think he was waiting for me? Like, waiting for me to come to England before he left?" Loïc looks to me.

I shake my head with a small smile. "I don't think it sounds silly at all. He was your last living relative. I think, on some level, he was waiting for you. He waited a long time to make sure you were okay. Once he saw that you were, he was free to let go." My voice cracks with emotion.

"Yeah." Loïc nods. He pulls me into his side, and we lie back down on the bed. "He was free to let go."

"Now, they can all be together," I say in a whisper.

Loïc runs his hand up and down my back. "That's a good thing."

"It is."

"I'm glad you're here with me."

"I'm always going to be with you, Loïc. We're no longer fucked up; we're just together. Right?"

"We're just together," he agrees.

I hear the smile in Loïc's voice, and I'm sure he's remembering what I told him so long ago. He kisses my head and pulls me in tighter.

The girl I was when I promised that had no idea of the gravity of those simple words. That girl was still learning what was truly important in life, what loss could do to a person, and what love truly meant.

The past couple of years have been full of ups and downs, incredible highs and devastating lows. As is evident from just the past hour, I know that life is going to continue to hand both Loïc and me joy and sadness.

That's kind of the nature of the game. Life is about balance, and to truly live it requires one to experience the plethora of emotions it brings.

I realize there will be hard times ahead just as there will be periods of complete bliss. Yet what I know deep down in my soul is that I've been given the gift of experiencing it all with Loïc by my side.

We will spend our lives together, experiencing all sorts of firsts, and I'm going to cherish each and every one.

EPILOGUE

London

> *"Today is the exact opposite of
> the wedding of my dreams. It's better."*
> —London Berkeley

Every little girl dreams of her perfect wedding. Throughout my childhood, I spent countless hours planning this day. I knew exactly what I wanted, every detail from the crystal vases that would hold elaborate floral displays at each table down to the brand of cutlery I wanted my guests eating with. I envisioned my hair, my dress, the music, the flowers, the colors...all of it.

Today is the exact opposite of the wedding of my dreams. It's better.

Parties end. It's what follows the celebration that matters. That's the good stuff. The wedding's great, but it's the *life* that counts. I can guarantee that the life I'll have with Loïc will be better than anything I dreamed.

True love isn't something you can imagine until you have it.

Staring back at me is the reflection of a woman I never knew existed but one that I'm so proud to be. I've always loved myself, but my self-worth goes beyond simple love now. For me, love was a given, but I had to work for that pride, and it's an awesome feeling. Life really is what you make of it, and I've strived to make sure I'm living a good one.

My hair falls around my shoulders in long brunette waves, covering the straps of my ivory gown. I touch the floral clip holding up a lock of hair. It was first worn by my great-grandmother in the 1920s, then my grandma, and then my mom. All the women who wore it have had long, happy marriages, and I'm about to be one of them. It's my *something old*, and I cherish it.

My mother's reflection appears behind me. Her eyes shine with happiness. "You are a stunning bride, London. Simply stunning."

"Thank you, Mom."

My mother and I had a few disputes during the initial planning stages of this wedding. With Georgia being the unpredictable free spirit that she is, my mom has always counted on me to have the big, traditional wedding extravaganza, including the crazy planning experience.

But I didn't give it to her in the way she wanted.

I no longer coveted the wedding that would cost more than my family's entire home. My mom was unpleased when I chose a dress off the rack instead of having one custom-made by a famous designer. But all of that lavishness seemed unimportant.

I have a few simple wishes for today. I want to feel pretty. I want to be surrounded by close family and friends. I want to officially promise Loïc forever.

And, finally, I want today to be full of quality time, laughs, and tons of love.

That's all.

I'm about to get everything I never knew I wanted—my happily ever after. And that brings an immense amount of gratitude with it, making me realize what's truly important.

I turn away from the mirror and toward my mother.

"You were right; the dress is perfect," my mother says. Her eyes glisten with tears as she squeezes my hands in hers.

"Isn't it?" I agree with a giant grin. My dress is simple, feminine, and flowy. It's the quintessential dress for a beach wedding.

"Oh my gosh!" Paige's excited voice sounds through the room. "You're so beautiful, London." She pulls me into a hug and holds me tight. Leaning back, she grabs my shoulders and looks me in the eyes. "I am so happy for you."

I smile at my best friend. "Thank you."

I think it's rare for people to feel pure happiness for someone else. So often, compliments and well wishes are painted with a stroke of jealousy. I don't think it's a bad or malicious fact. It's simply human nature. With a true friend, like Paige, who has such a kind heart, there is no internal *but* to her statement. She's not thinking, *I'm so happy for you, but...I wish it were me. Where's my soul mate? When will it be my turn?* She's just happy for me.

Friends that can give you a compliment without thinking of a *but* are treasures. And I'm lucky enough to have three of them standing up with me today.

Behind Paige are Kate and Georgia in their pale pink dresses that resemble mine, except for the color. My girls are elegant, carefree, and gorgeous, all at once. With our wavy locks and long dresses, we are four Greek goddesses.

"How's Loïc?" I ask Georgia.

"Happy," she answers with a warm smile.

My heart clenches with her response. "Me, too," I agree.

"I can tell. Happiness is just radiating from you." She takes my hand in hers and squeezes gently. "Are you ready? It's about that time."

"I *so* am." There isn't anything I want more than to promise Loïc that I'll love him till death do us part.

"I'm going to go take my place. I love you, baby girl." My mom leans in for another hug.

"Love you, too, Mom."

When she leaves the small space that we're using as our makeshift bridal room, the elegant music from the string quartet is carried in on the breeze of the salty sea air.

"Oh, they sound great," Paige says.

"They do, and that's our cue." Kate grins.

Butterflies are dancing with glee within my belly. "Okay, let's grab bouquets."

We take our bundles of beautiful flowers out of their vases. The multihued pink bouquets look great up against the bridesmaid dresses. Georgia hands me mine as my dad joins us.

He smiles down at me, his eyes shining with joy. He extends his bent elbow out, and I thread my arm through it.

"We'll see you at the end," Georgia says as the girls line up to start their procession down the aisle.

"Okay." I nod.

After a moment, when it's just me and my dad, he turns to the side and kisses me on the cheek. "You are the most beautiful bride I've ever seen, and I'm so happy for you."

"I love you, Daddy."

"I love you, too," he answers.

We exit the room and position ourselves at the center of the aisle.

I pull in a deep breath. My lips quiver as I attempt to hold back the tears. At the end of the shell-lined aisle, across the sand, Loïc is standing proudly in his military dress uniform. The beach behind our cottage, here in England, is the perfect backdrop for our wedding.

The string quartet changes songs, indicating my turn to venture down the aisle. As I pass our closest family and friends in one of our most favorite places on earth, I just can't wrap my mind around how fortunate I am. But it's Loïc's face that breaks the dam keeping my tears at bay. I can no longer hold in the emotion as it floods from me.

We made it. After so much heartache...we've arrived to our happily ever after. It's real. It's happening. It's such a gift.

I don't know if Loïc and I were fated to be with each other. Perhaps it was destiny and meant to be all along. Or maybe we are just two imperfect people who fit together perfectly. It could have been fate or plain luck that brought us together, but regardless, it was Loïc and I that kept us together.

Ours isn't a fairy-tale romance, but it is a love story. No one can help the way they were raised. Our life together didn't come easy. We had to work for it. But maybe that's why I value it so much. I know where we came from, and I know what it took to get here. And I know, now that I have this love, I'll never let it go.

So, when I look to Loïc now, it's with all of that knowledge in my heart. As his beautiful eyes gleam with unconditional love, I feel a mountain of gratitude weighing on my soul.

My dad places my hand in Loïc's, and our eyes lock together. I could get lost in his eyes. I could dive right in and never surface from their blue depths. Right now, they burn through me with the intensity of a love that promises forever.

Loïc rubs his thumb across the skin of my hand in small circles. He smiles, and it's a full-on devastating event that renders me helpless to take in anything else but him, my guy.

We exchange vows.

We slide on rings.

We get lost in our bubble of bliss, oblivious to those around us.

Loïc leans in to kiss me. When he's a mere breath away, he halts and whispers against my lips, "I've discovered a new flaw."

"What's that?"

"I can never function again in a world where you aren't mine." His low voice is raspy and full of emotion.

"From the moment I met you, I've been yours. My greatest flaw is that my heart will never be able to love anyone else the way I love you."

His fingers splay across the small of my back as he pulls me closer to him. "Good thing you'll never have to," he answers huskily.

"Damn good thing." I inhale his breath. "Now, kiss me, husband."

"Gladly, wife."

Loïc captures my mouth with his. I pour everything into the kiss because that's what Loïc is to me...*everything*.

EPILOGUE

Loïc

> *"Our life has love, beauty, and purpose.*
> *I can't think of anything better."*
> —*Loïc Berkeley*

"All done. The last paint can is stacked up on the shelf in the garage. We are unpacked, decorated, and organized. We are officially moved in," London says with a sigh of glee. She places a mug of coffee on the small table before plopping down in the lounge chair beside me.

"Good job, babe." I reach out my hand, and she takes it, entwining her fingers through mine.

We sit out on our three-seasons porch that overlooks the rolling hills of the Great Smoky Mountains. The trees that blanket the vast hills range in color from the deep green of the pines to the burnt orange, golds, and reds of the others. Autumn here is nothing short of breathtaking.

Life for the Berkeleys is awesome.

London and I chose to buy a house near the border of Tennessee and North Carolina. The natural splendor of the area was a huge deciding factor. It's stunning during all four seasons of the year. The array of outdoor activities, from skiing to white-water rafting, was also a big draw.

London and I both travel some with our jobs. She's a freelance writer for several papers, including the *New York Times*. She does all of her writing here but has to travel for research. If I'm not busy, I go with her. Both of the states that border our home have many VA medical centers. I keep busy with leading groups and traveling around the country, giving talks and raising awareness for issues affecting our veterans. London and I are also starting a nonprofit organization to help veterans battling PTSD in hopes of lowering the twenty-two-per-day suicide rate.

Our life has love, beauty, and purpose. I can't think of anything better.

"We're free next weekend, right?" I ask London.

"Yeah, we are."

"Oh, good. I thought we were. Sarah wants to visit."

"Oh, great!" London exclaims. "I miss Evan."

"Me, too." I grin, thinking about my adorable two-year-old nephew.

She takes a sip of coffee. "Is Dixon coming, too?"

"Yep, Dick can make it," I answer with a chuckle.

"Awesome. So, they're still doing well?"

"Yeah, Sarah says they're doing awesome."

Sarah and Dixon hooked up after our wedding this past spring and have been dating since. I'm so happy for both of them. Dixon is a great man, and he loves Sarah and Evan.

"Oh, look." London points toward the large oak tree behind our porch. "Poppy and Pooh are getting so big."

I look over to see our resident raccoon family climbing up the tree. London named the mama Priscilla, and her babies were named Poppy and Pooh. The babies have more than doubled in size since we first saw them when we moved in a couple of months ago.

"Yeah, they're not really babies anymore, are they?"

"I wonder how long they'll stay with Priscilla before they venture out on their own," London says.

"I'm not sure. Hopefully through the winter." I shrug.

"I need to place more food out to make sure they get really fat before hibernation. Raccoons hibernate, right?"

I smile wide, squeezing her hand in mine. "I think so. Don't worry; they're doing just fine. They're already pretty plump."

"I know, but more food won't hurt them."

We watch the mama and her babies until they disappear up the tree.

London lets go of my hand and turns on her side to face me. "So, what do you want to do today?"

"You," I respond simply.

London laughs and then flashes me an easy smile that makes my heart stutter. "Is that so?"

"It's definitely so."

"Well, I might be able to make that happen," she says with an alluring voice and burning eyes. She stands, leaving her chair, and straddles me in mine.

The casual morning atmosphere has disappeared, leaving us in a fog of lust.

I feel her warm breath on my skin as her soft lips kiss up my neck until they reach my mouth. Kneading her back with my hands, I hold her close as my mouth ravishes hers.

243

Our lips collide. Our tongues clash. Shared moans resonate.

I love this woman more every day, and just when I think I couldn't possibly love her more, the sun rises, bringing a new day, and my heart is full of even more adoration for my wife.

London rips her mouth from mine and makes quick work of removing our clothes, leaving us bare and ready. Reaching my hands out in front of me, I smooth my palms across her skin, branding her with my touch. Every inch of her body is so soft and insanely sexy. She drives me crazy every second of every day with how beautiful she is.

Biting her bottom lip, her eyes heavy, her hair tousled and sexy, she wastes no time. She firmly grabs me, placing me at her entrance, and slides down onto my shaft with an intoxicating groan of pleasure. My fingers squeeze her ass as she starts to move atop me.

The sounds of nature have faded away, giving voice to our panting, jagged and raw breaths, the slapping of our bodies coming together, and finally, to our moans of pleasure.

London collapses on top of me, her face against my chest. "Your heartbeat's so strong," she sighs against my skin.

"Because it's beating for you," I answer with the truth.

In this ever-moving sea of life, I'm an imperfect vessel, unable to predict what the next wave will bring. There's only one thing I'm certain of. Regardless of where this life might take me, every wild beat of my flawed heart will be for London.

So long ago, as a scared little boy, I would wish to go to London where I could be happy. What I didn't realize then that I do now is that a place doesn't have the power to heal, but people do.

Salvation isn't found in geography but in love.

I was right to pray for London because it turns out that I needed her all along. I had to experience the overwhelming force of loving someone as much as I do her. It's that fierce love that enabled me to save myself.

Loving London is what makes me who I am. She's the only one who's ever penetrated deep into my heart.

Loving London saved me. And I'm going to spend the rest of my life showing her how very grateful I am.

DEAR READERS

I hope you loved reading Loïc and London's story as much as I adored writing it. There are so many incredible books out there, and I am truly grateful that you chose to read one of mine. I wouldn't be living this dream without you. Thank you from the bottom of my heart!

Loving London touched on a very real topic—depression and PTSD in our veterans. Entire novels could be written on this subject. It was merely a part of the plot in this one because, ultimately, this was a love story.

I have nothing but the utmost respect and gratitude for our military. My grandfather, father, stepfather, brother, and many dear friends have served or continue to serve in the armed forces.

When I was in sixth grade, I had to interview a veteran for a school project. I chose to talk to my grandpa about his time in the Korean War. I will never forget the way he broke down, sobbing in tears, during one of his stories. My grandpa is one of the strongest men I know, yet after marriage, five kids, seventeen grandkids, and the decades of time that had passed, he was still reduced to tears when he spoke about the friends he'd lost in the war. War affects those involved in ways I can't even begin to imagine.

I have seen what the wars in Afghanistan and Iraq have done to some of my friends. I've seen marriages and families fall apart because soldiers don't come back the same. Losing their families is a heartbreaking reality for many veterans.

There was this boy from my community. He was one of those kids who was always smiling, the constant jokester and everyone's friend. Just an all-around great kid. Upon graduating, he joined the Marines. Now, four years later, this past week, he became one of the twenty-two suicides per day by taking his own life.

I'm no expert in this subject, but I don't think one has to be to know that there's a problem. There are some things that man is not meant to do or see, and when our soldiers come back, they need help. A man or woman who served their country shouldn't be homeless or feel that the only way to end their suffering is to take their life.

There are many organizations trying to help our veterans. A simple Google search will produce lots of ways in which you can get involved in your own community. Raise awareness. Reach out to anyone you know who might be struggling.

People helping people…it's the best. ❤

Thank you for reading.

Sending you lots of love,

Ellie ❤

RESOURCES

These are some organizations dedicated to helping veterans of Iraq and Afghanistan with PTSD and depression.

The Headstrong Project

www.facebook.com/HeadstrongProject

The Wounded Warrior Project

www.woundedwarriorproject.org/programs

Freedom Alliance

http://freedomalliance.org

Healing Warrior Hearts

http://starfishfound.org/veterans

National Coalition for Homeless Veterans

http://nchv.org

Mission 22

www.mission22.com

Stop Soldier Suicide

http://stopsoldiersuicide.org

National Center for PTSD

www.ptsd.va.gov

ACKNOWLEDGMENTS

In every one of my acknowledgment sections, I get quite wordy when expressing my love to all the amazing people in my life. I am so fortunate to have this life I've been given. I have a wonderful husband, healthy and happy children, an astonishing extended family, the best mother in the world, and friends who would do anything for me. I am so blessed and grateful to be surrounded by so much love that I want to shout it from the rooftops.

A special shout-out will always go to my siblings, who were my first soul mates. You will find them in every story I write because so much of what I know of love has come from them. One of my biggest wishes for my children is that they will always love each other unconditionally and fiercely, the way my siblings and I love each other.

To my beta readers, blogger friends, author friends, and readers who message me—You all are so awesome. Seriously, each of you is a gift, and you have helped me in invaluable different ways. I love you all so much. XOXO

A huge hug is being sent out into the world in honor of Angela and Elle, two women who love and support me in so many ways. I love you both, big time!

> Angela, my cupcake—I've said it before, and I will say it again. I love you big time, like hard-core, intense love! I can't thank you enough for all you do for me on a daily basis! I am so truly blessed to know you. ♥

> Elle—I love you for so many reasons! I especially love how you make me laugh when I need it! Thank you for loving and supporting me. You are such an amazing person. Thank you for all you do to help me! I am so grateful. ♥

This book especially wouldn't be what it is without three incredible women.

> Gayla—Thank you for taking time out of your busy life to help me, no matter what I need. You are so smart and talented. I love your feedback and your honesty. You are a blessing, and I love you more than I could ever express.

> Tammi—I've said it before, and I will say it again. I will forever continue to write as long as you continue to read because your feedback alone is enough. *You get me.* Thank you for being you because you are perfect. I live for your comments and feedback. Not only do you fill my heart

with so much gratitude, but you also make me a better writer. *Tight Hugs* I freaking love you!

Amy, my BBFFL—What can I say that I haven't already said? You know how much I love you! I have cherished your support from the beginning. Eight novels later, you continue to bless me with your feedback and support. You get me and my writing. You make my books better. You are one of the kindest and most supportive people I know. I love you to pieces! ♥

To my cover artist, Regina Wamba from Mae I Design and Photography—Thank you! Your work inspires me. You are a true artist, and I am so grateful to now have eight of your covers. People do judge a book by its cover, so thank you for making mine *gorgeous*! XO

To my editor and interior designer, Jovana Shirley from Unforeseen Editing—You are, simply put, the best. Your talent, professionalism, and the care you take with my novels are worth way more than I could ever afford to pay you. Finding you was a true gift, one that I hope to always have on this journey. Thank you from the bottom of my heart for not only making my words pretty, but for also making the interior of the book beautiful. Thank you for always fitting me in! I am so grateful for you and everything you have done to make this book the best it can be. XOXO

To the bloggers—I adore you! Out of the kindness of your hearts, so many of you have reached out and helped me promote my books. There are seriously great people in this blogger community, and I am humbled by your support. Truly, thank you! Because of you, indie authors get their stories out. Thank you for supporting all authors and the great stories they write.

Lastly, to the readers—I want to thank you so very much. Thank you for reading my stories and loving my words! I wouldn't be living this dream without you. Thank you from the bottom of my heart!

You can connect with me on several places, and I would love to hear from you.

Find me on Facebook:
www.facebook.com/EllieWadeAuthor

Find me on Twitter: @authorelliewade

Visit my website: www.elliewade.com

Remember, the greatest gift you can give an author is a review. If you feel so inclined, please leave a review on the various retailer sites. It doesn't have to be fancy. A couple of sentences would be awesome!

I could honestly write a whole book about everyone in this world whom I am thankful for. I am blessed in so many ways, and I am beyond grateful for this beautiful life. XOXO

Forever,

Ellie ♥

ABOUT THE AUTHOR

Ellie Wade resides in southeast Michigan with her husband, three young children, and two dogs. She has a master's in education from Eastern Michigan University, and she is a huge University of Michigan sports fan. She loves the beauty of her home state, especially the lakes and the gorgeous autumn weather. When she is not writing, she is reading, snuggling up with her kids, or spending time with family and friends. She loves traveling and exploring new places with her family.

Made in the USA
Middletown, DE
18 October 2017